S0-ACV-336

other Books by Erika Lopez

HOOCHIE MAMA
THE OTHER WHITE MEAT

FLAMING IGUANAS
an Illustrated all-girl Road Novel THing

Lap Dancing for Mommy
★ ★ TENDER STORIES of Disgust, Blame, + Inspiration

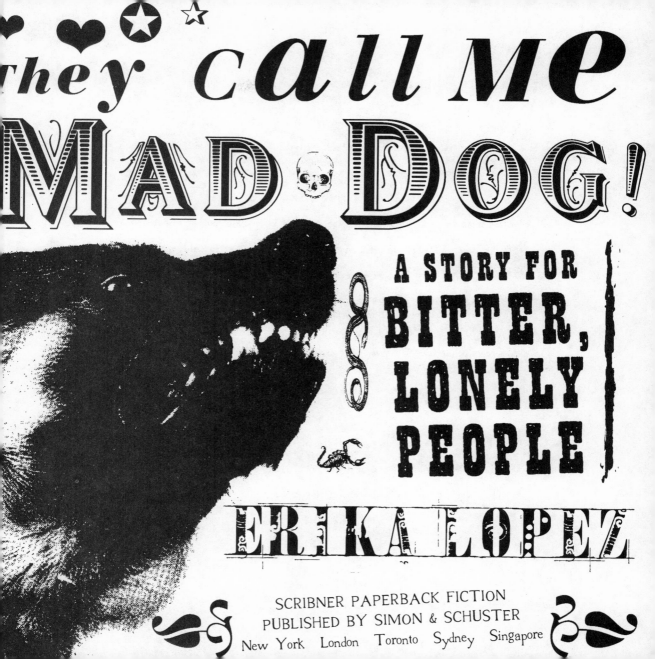

SCRIBNER PAPERBACK FICTION
Simon & Schuster, Inc.
Rockefeller Center
1230 Avenue of the Americas
New York, NY 10020

This book is a work of fiction. Names, characters, places, and incidents either are products
of the author's imagination or are used fictitiously. Any resemblance to actual events
or locales or persons, living or dead, is entirely coincidental.

Copyright © 1998 by Erika Lopez

All rights reserved, including the right of reproduction in whole or in part in any form.

Erika Lopez P.O. Box 410011/San Francisco, CA 94141/or ErikaLopez.com

First Scribner Paperback Fiction edition 2000

SCRIBNER PAPERBACK FICTION and design are trademarks of Macmillan Library Reference USA, Inc.,
used under license by Simon & Schuster, the publisher of this work.

Designed by Erika Lopez, with special guest star, Paul Smith/and an appearance by Devil Girl™,
which appears courtesy of R. Crumb. (For more information about Devil Girl Choco-Bars
and other cool stuff, call 1-800-365-7465/or KitchenSink.com)

Manufactured in the United States of America

1   3   5   7   9   10   8   6   4   2

The Library of Congress has cataloged the Simon & Schuster edition as follows:
Lopez, Erika.
They call me Mad Dog! : a story for bitter, lonely people / Erika Lopez.
p.   cm.
Sequel to: Flaming iguanas.
I. Title.
PS3562.0672T48   1998
813'.54—dc21   98-43002
CIP

ISBN 0-684-84941-0
0-684-84942-9 (Pbk)

I'd like to give a big round of applause to
Sandra "Lady" May, "Big Daddy" Bob Mecoy,
and "Flammer Boy" Mark Lammers,
because without them
I would've had nothing to do
except watch thirties porn,
wear slippers all day,
and yell at happy little children.

Together, they're like the three tenors
who wrote the songs that make the whole world
sing.

And today's word is "perineum."

The in-between place that t'aint neither here nor there. It is not only a useless thing like pizza crust that sex manuals tell you to lick when you don't know what to do next. No. It's a metaphor for a state of mind, a way of life, an approach to sexuality, and a way of enjoying limbo when you haven't got a clue what to do next and it ends up being a very nice place to put your tongue for a while.

"Perineum."

Open your legs and your mind to that place in between.

Her fake mustache hadn't fooled them, so she very subtly pulled her turtleneck up over her nose so she'd just look like Bazooka Joe in a hurry. But they saw through everything. They saw through the blue eye shadow, the green fingernails, the salty sweat and atomic yellow sweater pulled down past her waist, over her hips, and through the woods, past the morning's coffee, and over her fears of appearing on the Rosie O'Donnell show.

Ten more minutes and she'd be sitting next to Rosie, helping to perpetuate the myth that Rosie was heterosexual so parents wouldn't mind her talking to their unadopted children so much.

It was a crispy, crunchy autumn morning. On her way to the studio she saw people waving flimsy signs by the entrance. Signs for her, signs against her.

The ten minutes passed, sneezed, pissed, frittered away. According to Warhol, the girl in the turtleneck sweater would have five minutes left. Five minutes of fame to set the record straight and say hello to her mother.

She thought the death of John Denver would make her mom call her this morning, but it hadn't. It made her want to call her mother and see if she was alright, but time . . . there wasn't enough time, never enough time in New York to even yak up your brunch and chastise yourself for not being in a better relationship.

0-0001-0

Twenty years ago, her mom used to spend entire evenings bitching about men with her friends. They'd start the evening off with a gallon of wine, a crackling fire, and a half-inch stack of records on the turntable. By the time they turned the ten-pound stack of records over, the fire would be nothing more than a pile of Christmas lights, and they'd be thinning the last of the wine down with rubbing alcohol, slurring, and giving each other naked massages on the frizzy white carpeting.

I am I said, I am I cried, Neil Diamond; turtleneck woman, Helen Reddy; Simply Barbra; *One Less Bell to Answer* in the Fifth Dimension; the sad and isolated Carpenters; Gordon Lightfoot; and of course: John Denver, who moved a whole generation to appreciate the mountains of West Virginia, thank God for being country boys, and drive drunk in Colorado.

The girl in the turtleneck knew all the words by heart. Put a gun to her temple and she'll sing a "We've Only Just Begun" that's emotionally wrenching enough to convince an advanced cancer patient that he'll be rolling his wheelchair back and forth over all his friends' graves.

Gun? The Carpenters? A wheelchair? Sounds more like one of those British fetishes Prince Charles might get into once he tires of wishing to be a premenopausal woman's tampon, but keep your judgment in your front pocket and tell someone else you're just glad to see them because even though we've only just begun, we've all heard it before.

0-0002-0

But how did she get what little rhythm she did manage to get? Just enough rhythm to keep her from getting her ass kicked in the Bronx through the ruthless age of adolescent disco, just enough rhythm to convince little white kids she could kick their little flat behinds? Why of course, she had to run next door to the obese, sweaty-pink couple surrounded by big boxes of Cepacol mouthwash samples for a copy of "The Beat Goes On."

A producer jogged up to the nervous daughter in the turtleneck sweater as if his shoelaces were tied together, and the daughter stopped humming her history. Headset clipped to his head and a notebook in his hand, he nervously whispered, "Okay, okay—Mrs. Dog, are you ready?"

She quietly hissed "*Misssss*" at him as she licked her lips and wet her mental bed, before she blacked out and sauntered onto the stage with tingly armpits and a monogamous smile.

If I were writing a novel, this is how I would've started it. I would've gone on to tell you that my appearance on her show inspired Rosie O'Donnell to say she was gay, and proud of it, and that I further inspired Catherine Deneuve to spontaneously call in and openly proclaim she really *did* like kissing Susan Sarandon and that she was really so, so sorry about suing that lezzbian *Deneuve* magazine for using her name . . .

. . . and how, how could she *ever, ever* make it up to everyone.

If this were a novel, Rosie would've invited her over for dinner. The doorbell would chime to the tune of Doris Day's "Secret Love," and Chastity Bono would be at the door carrying framed photos of Hollywood pussy mashers and dead muff divers.

Not five minutes later, the doorbell would ring again, and my old gym teacher would show up fashionably late on the arm of the down-and-out Sandra Bernhard. My gym teacher would be dressed as Agnes Moorehead *because the changing of the homosexual Darrens was such an important time for so many of us.* Then they'd all turn to Sandra Bernhard and give her a big group hug and tell her it was alright because, *oh honey, careers have their ups and downs.*

Soon after, Shirley MacLaine would crash the party in her *Children's Hour* character and threaten to hang herself in the bathroom, and after they talked her out of it, they would all laugh that fake Prozac laughter, like it was the end of another TV show.

0 - 0005 - 0

Then they'd sit down to a genitally reminiscent dinner of oysters, tacos, and peaches. No, I repeat, no asparagus, even though it's an aphrodisiac, because lesbians can't have sex after asparagus unless they want to gag each other. Boys, you'd do well to remember that too if you want to play vacuum cleaner salesman after dinner.

And then they'd all have sex together and Penny Marshall, Rosie's Kmart/director friend, would accidentally pop by and end up filming the whole thing as a hands-across-America porn video for lesbians to help support the cure for AIDS, since nursing all their friends to death in the eighties wasn't nearly enough.

But I'm not writing a novel. This is real life.
Harsh, fluorescent-cold real life, complete with its occasional little spankings, and Catherine Deneuve is not sorry.

You may have noticed that nowadays we have to choose whether to have a life or a lifestyle. In a lifestyle life, shiny gay magazines try to convince lesbians to wear angora sweaters for special events and try to teach women to not seduce each other while wearing graying bras held together with safety pins. But in real life lesbians buy more flannel than Alaskans, even the lesbians who live in Africa and Florida. It's just a thing, because if you're gonna get turned down, for Pete's sake, you don't want it to be because she thought you were straight.

In real life, a lesbian you knew probably listened to the Indigo Girls until you couldn't even stand secondary colors green and purple, but that's okay. Because it's all about sisterhood, anyway, isn't it?

In real life lesbians have dogs. Big dogs. Big dogs that behave because lesbians have control issues, and they love to jam their boot down on someone's neck and talk all about it. Because in real life, lesbians just love to process issues like jackals gnawing on baby gazelles in the Serengeti.

And in real life this is a story about my search for the perfect place between New Age passivity and knife-slicing feelings. Trying to find not only the yin and the yang, the top and the bottom, left-right, butch-femme, democratic-republican, but the fluffy cream filling in between. No whiny Twinkie defense for me, but the Little Debby way of dealing with scary little things like gouging-eye-socket rage and experiencing the taste of white trash and the sugar rush that comes with it.

No one seems to be real sure about how to do anger. It's still like the last frontier where you can find your strength, your power, your insanity, your inhumanity, and mostly your fears, but ultimately who you are. And if you plan some kind of expedition into yourself and ride a wave all the way in front of the proverbial mirror, you should come out alright and still be able to ride through the storm and save the princess just in time before the credits roll.

We give tissues for tears, we give hugs for accomplishments, and we hand over teddy bears in the dark. But when you get angry, some people cower and think it's all over between you, while others threaten to drive powder blue Cadillacs through your front door. Therapists tell you to sit and feel the electricity of anger burning through your extremities, while religion tells you to just go do something nice for someone. Give them a corn cob duck.

Although I ultimately wanted to find myself somewhere in the creamy-filled center between the two, I didn't start out that way. Years of therapy telling me to sit still and feel the electric surges of fury, and many dog-eared daily affirmation books later, telling me to let it go like a little bird. *Set it free! Set it free!* But my bird always came back to peck my eyes out, so there I was in real life, starting from the flashier side. The side with loud slaps, big red mouths, macaroni and cheese, and glitter. Lots and lots of glitter.

Because although there might be that sisterhood thing poking up its little fallopian tentacles everywhere, that gets tedious and boring the way most NAACP stuff gets, so then it really all comes down to simply looking good, doesn't it? Lots and lots of glitter. Puerto Ricans and drag queens knew it all the time.

But the Puerto Rican drag queens never, ever warned me that, *careful—girlfriends make objects appear larger than they really are.*

So let me take you back to a day when I was wearing a sweaty black acrylic ski mask on my face in the dead of summer, screeching around the barrio corners of San Francisco in a friend's champagne-colored Lexus 4x4, looking for a woman named Hooter *Mujer/*a woman who done me wrong. Harmonica wrong. A bad, bad woman who took my hand, led me to the sapphic muff-diving waters and made me feel like I was a filling up and spilling over lezzbian. A woman who finger-fucked my aorta/made like the Bronx and played handball with my heart.

I lifted the bottom of the damp mask to the top of my lip and lit a cigarette, and there she was at the other end of the block unlocking her new car door at a perfect and unaware 9:15 in the morning. I dropped my foot on the gas like 1929 and I jammed my hand into the glove box/pulled out a can of Reddi Wip and a small 2x4.

Methamphetamine jitters shimmied throughout my arms and the acid burn of good old-fashioned revenge gurgled up the back of my stretchy little deep throat like a garden fountain.

When I screamed to a stop, she looked up like a cow, like a deer, like a rabbit, like a skunk, like anything caught in the headlights of a very, very bad day.

A good day might start off with juice, toast, and maybe an egg or two. Maybe a good day starts off because you know you're not bouncing checks, maybe you were fucked with long fingers or lightly tickled in a funny way by a Fragonard Pekingese this morning. Maybe for you it started off with an encouraging spanking because you're into that kind of thing and you've been a very bad, bad little girl. Maybe a good day starts off real well because you're a compulsive eater and for once you've actually got scrapings of ice cream left for breakfast.

But when you're in love, it doesn't matter whether you eat real eggs or just somebody else's bodily fluids for breakfast and it doesn't even matter whether it's first-thing-Monday-morning, because every day's Sunday in the park with George.

The year before I hit thirty I thought I was a used-up thing with vibrator calluses. Too old and crispy like *chicharrón* to fall in love, but like most fried pork skin, I fell in love against all the odds with my late father's business partner, Hodie, whom I called Hooter. They'd had a sex-toy business together.

My sister and I inherited my late father's half of the business, but we cashed it in. My sister wanted to pay for a breast reduction so she could do things like lie on her stomach without cutting holes in the bed, and I wanted to get a decent place to live in the city so I'd have enough room to make fake penises without getting a job right away.

About a thousand square feet. That's what I had in a city that never lets anyone get away with a good deal, so I was bound to get fucked in some other way.

I listened to so many stories about *before*. It seemed like the best of San Francisco was *before* when you could have sex with a stranger and lope away with your first case of herpes and a whole lot of plans for the future/*before* when you weren't lying through your teeth that one week's salary really could cover your monthly rent on an apartment application.

But all the hippies who once raised their fists in the air without deodorant, tried to save the world while bowing to Indian gurus, and paid seventy bucks a *month* for a decent apartment, were now the middle-aged yuppies who had begun sprouting tagua nut button shirts and turning into landlords. Landlords who thought $70 a day was a reasonable rent.

They just wanted to save the world, buy it, rent it back to us, and balance out the whole exploit/save thing. The idea, they say, is to die at the exact moment it's all gone. Your bank account and the ozone layer. But it gets a little trickier when you're freezing everything to enjoy for when you've got the time. Organic vegetables, sperm, eggs, and yourself./I just got one word for ya: cryogenics, baby.

Ah, greed ...

Q-Q013-

The eighties has left behind a huge skid mark of HIV-positive blood and a coffee generation nervous about cooties and the first of the month/cynically chasing the idea of romantic love around like it's *Rumpelstiltskin! Rumpelstiltskin! Rumpelstiltskin!*

Unfortunately, Rumpelstiltskin has left the building.

San Francisco's also full of happy and gay people in their forties with the friendship memories of extremely old people, so they start nonprofit organizations with clever acronyms that took months to figure out titles for, LLEGO, CAPA, BAR, NOHARMM, PFLAG, and jog around the city, tossing Ziploc bags of bubble-gum-flavored latex things to people wondering how to pay their rent and have sex without getting all wet.

Living here made me greedy. I wanted my own place to live so no one was finding the cure for their own death on my rent check. The problem is that I'm seeing just how the Indians got pushed out of America. What the fuck happened?

When they came to evict the Indians, I wasn't Indian, so I didn't stand up for them. When they came to evict the Palestinians, I wasn't Palestinian, so I didn't stand up for them. And when they came to evict the gays who made entire neighborhoods hip, well, actually, I think all the older gays bought their houses with all that dual income they've got. Anyway, by the time they got around to evicting me, no one was left to stand up for me because all the artists had already moved to the East Bay.

A thousand square feet. I was so lucky to find such a place in a city where the word "fag" is a compliment.

I lived in the flattest, sunny Mexican part of the city, where janitors still owned property, and their houses were painted like candy in a bowl: shiny purple, swimming pool blue, Technicolor orange, and nah, don't worry, the trim doesn't *really* have to match. *That's one of those urban myths, Juan.* Got any navy in that can? Any canary yellow in your basement from that job over on Silver Avenue?

It was a daring neighborhood, paintings on buildings, bright fruit in the gutters, and emotionally wrenching *ranchera* music everywhere. If you put a paper bag over your head, you would've sworn you were walking down a sidewalk made of broken hearts.

Sure, sure, human urine stained these squishy, broken-hearted sidewalks, dogs routinely rolled in homeless human shit, but isn't that a small price to pay to live in the kind of neighborhood where "Braun cappuccino maker" isn't the punch line to some yuppie story?

Once I was in one of San Francisco's boutique neighborhoods, Union Street—even saying it makes me shudder—walking behind a fashionably emaciated, well-tailored couple on maybe their second date. He had his camel-hair arm around her and the punch line to a story was a Braun cappuccino maker.

And even more amazing is that she tossed her overpriced casual hair back and *laughed* at the punch line.

I'm afraid it's one of those things I'll never forget as long as I live, because it was one of those shameful moments where you want to scream, "Oh my God! *I'm* not an American, *they* are! Kill *them!*"

Yes, here in the Mission District you're more likely to hear rumors about how homeboys give their pit bulls hand jobs in order to bond, and that's why I like it here, because that's just the kind of gal I am.

But I'm afraid none of us are safe and Braun coffeemaker jokes are the wave of the future. But at least *here* people can wait for another earthquake to make expensive people scatter back east. What can you wish for in Manhattan? Another silly little blackout with days of looting, or a late-summer garbage strike?

I lucked out because I didn't have to donate someone else's kidney to get the place. The guy who lived here last was a Quaker boy named John, who was also from Philadelphia, now moving back east to New York with his frizzy-headed girlfriend who wanted to make it as a *fabulous* New York artist. She didn't seem to get too excited over things like they do in California. She had just the right amount of half-lidded ennui, so if she was gonna make it anywhere she just might make it there.

It was so cool to meet another Quaker guy from Philadelphia. We found that we both lived in West Virginia when we were kids and we also went to the same art school. He had the same ennui thing going on, too. Maybe that's why these two were lovers, because then neither one would whine that the other didn't care. They just understood about getting too emotionally messy. But the more I chatted with him, the more I chalked his ennui up to being a Quaker guy.

See, you'd find that Quaker guys are generally quite masculine, and they usually have to be because they're always lugging crates of cans to homeless shelters or building houses for folks in the Appalachian Mountains.

So I guess what passed for ennui was the peacefulness that came from fighting the urge to not evict anybody.

In fact, he said I could have his place.

It was a great old little low-ceilinged building that had been a workshop before people stopped making things in this town. My favorite thing was the long, wide, unfinished wood planks stretching all the way to the back kitchen. They creaked when you walked like you two were having a good conversation. The kitchen used to be the back office, and there was still a cut-out window for doing business.

All around the place I had scattered many different chairs so you could sit wherever you wanted. Chairs with spoked backs, chipping paint; chairs with ripped caning; chairs with family pictures glued all over them; and my favorite, an inexpensive chair from Sweden that resembled a classic design from the fifties.

There was even a chair in the bathroom so you could sit and talk to someone on the toilet. In the kitchen, you could sit as soon as you came in the back door, if you were tired and wanted to wait before you went any farther. By the front door, there were three chairs so that up to three guests could sit at the same time and remove their shoes.

As I was approaching thirty, I was refining the obsessions that will probably become full-blown by the time I'm well into my middle age.

I used to take the bus and see people sneeze into their hands and then touch the rails. New, unsuspecting people would put their hands in the same spot. If that doesn't make you wash your hands before you even put down your mail, nothing will. Granted, on public transportation, you're lucky if tuberculosis patients actually cover their mouths.

And after living in the Mission District, with all the urine, spit, blood, and sticky condoms congealing on the sidewalks, it takes almost ten minutes to realize taking off shoes at home is the way to avoid all the evil, screaming voices from outer space in your head.

A n y h o w, enough pulling back the flap on my impending obsessive-compulsive disorder: my place had big storefront windows covered with black curtains and I left it that way. The place was dark. Dark, but cozy. The good thing was that you didn't notice dirt much. The better thing was that it smelled vaguely spicy and a little human.

John had built a small spiral staircase up to the attic area, and made it like a bedroom. So I followed his example and did my work downstairs. My important fake-penis work.

I had to face it: fake penises were my calling. Vaginas just weren't funny. They come out flat and look like you're trying to make some kind of antiquated feminist statement, which is never hilarious. Maybe female reproductive systems could be sort of funny, because they look like a cartoon rabbit on all the posters in the gynecologist's office, and that conjures up images of Bugs Bunny with that carrot—but, see, then you're back to phallic stuff with the carrot.

Things that stick out are funny. Breasts stick out, and they're really only funny to guys in bars or twelve-year-old boys with obscene pewter toys. But penises look funnier the way they just hang there dangling alone like flabby little Christmas meats. As long as they're not pumped full of blood and poking at things, they're as harmless and cute as a naked little mole rat burrowing a hole to call home.

So I set up four sawhorses, laid a couple of old doors on top, and started making fake penises.

Then I photographed them and made many copies at the drugstore across the street. I sent packets of them everywhere: New York galleries, where sex is nailed to a stark white wall and called cutting edge; L.A. sex shops, where sex is scraped off the floor and sprayed down with a shot of Lysol and handed in paper bags to movie stars in the dark of night; and San Francisco sex shops, where the sun shines in, the carpet's clean and purple, and tourists try to pretend they do this *all the time* back home.

I started off selling them through Hooter's sex-toy business, and they were pretty much a hit right away because evidently I wasn't the only one tired of lavender dolphin penises and penises shaped like rabbits with rotating gum-ball machines in the middle. Sex with animals is where I draw the line (at least right now), and it even gets weirder when you throw in gum-ball machines. Call me old-fashioned, but having sex with children's toys is one step too close to the *really* forbidden zone.

So in under four months, my Cher penises and Tribble penises were selling like frizzy poontang in the Old West. I was picking my teeth and wondering how much I wanted to expand and become the grande dame of fake penises.

Women who've made entire cottage industries out of extremely personal interests have always sort of given me the creeps.

And don't throw that "well, if it were a man" thing on me. Martha Stewart scares me more than Bill Gates ever could. If you've ever worked for a woman you may know what I mean, and I'm not trying to be fashionable like some new kind of backlash misogynistic feminist, either. I love women. Hey, some of my best friends are women. It's just that working for women or in a family-run business has instilled in me the fear of apple pie, self-help books, and genetic togetherness.

Some women want to catch up on thousands of years of getting men and children ready for the footlights. Now they want to rule the world with stern, nurturing smiles and cover the world with huge Venus flytraps.

Not me. I just wanted to fuck everyone with a thousand penises and write lipstick good-byes on medicine chests like so many before me.

Before I came to San Francisco I was somehow under the impression that men were historically the ones fucking women over, but that's just a whole lot of bad press. Give women the chance and they fuck each other over just as much, if not more. Women are just as bad as men, even though they're way better in bed. (The trouble is that they talk too much in the morning.) They fuck each other over and invite ex-girlfriends who cheated on them over for Thanksgiving. And between the new and old girlfriends sitting around the table, the act of carving the turkey becomes either erotic, painful, or infuriating. There's no escaping it. If you're going to fuck girls, that's the way it will be. Once you end up with a woman who knows what the hell she's doing in bed (unlike me), you'd also bark like a dog if it meant she'd come right back. Listen Paco, even lesbian sex at its flea-bitten *worst* is still pretty damn good because you'll *always* come, even when you thought you left your clit on some kitchen counter back in Africa.

Anyway, once I had gotten a firm bite from the art world, I strongly veered the penises directly into the gallery scene.

Hooter was busy with the sex-toy business, so I flew alone to New York for my first art opening, and met the two gallery directors. Two women with a brutal sense of humor and dried blood under their fingernails. I knew I'd be in good hands as long as I kept peroxide in my purse and a box of Band-Aids wedged under my armpit.

I kept getting their names confused. One's name was Mimi Feldperson and the other's name was Jenny Pie. They were both barely old enough to dot a tampon, but that's how it is in New York. New York is a fast track. Those dogs . . . They *bite.* They don't even bother barking. They start out young and hungry, dressed in black, cultivating that New York ennui thing where it always looks like they're in between yawns, hoping to God no one comes up behind them and suddenly tickles them in front of a photographer.

They were both short. Short women are scarier than tall, skinny women. Short women from New York can mentally zoom around you like little race cars, leaving you feeling like your skirt's blowing up, showing your underwear. And not in that sexy

Marilyn Monroe kind of way, either. In an orphan train line-up kind of way.

It wasn't hard to become really, really quiet and polite around them. That was the only way I could be sure they wouldn't have any of my blood under their nails.

At the first art opening, I constantly had people walking up to me saying hello and the two short gallery directors hovered around me, discreetly touching me with pieces of tape to take away the Nena kitty hair. I didn't get it until the opening was over and I saw a trash can full of hairy loops of masking tape.

I was grateful to the short New York women with the long nails, and I felt taken care of.

Anyway, that's not important: the show was a sellout and that's pretty much where this story begins: with my ominous Basquiat-like penis success.

I called her Hooter because she had awe-inspiring tits. They could complete a *New York Times* crossword puzzle in under a half hour and tell you how to push your own cleavage together and ask for *more.* You couldn't get much more real.

("Tits" sounds so vulgar though, doesn't it? Every time I say it I see a double-D cup woman who can't spell CAT, rubbing her tits in someone's face. The kind of woman who hears "tits" and instantly holds one up to her mouth like *$2.95 a minute big boy...*)

It seemed like Hooter and I were in love like a couple of Mexican street dogs and for the first six months we fucked every day, only she did most of the finger-fucking because she knew what she was doing better than I. Of course. I had absolutely no finesse. Of course. I still had some problem turning my hand sideways at crucial moments, and the whole rhythm thing . . . I just got too thrown off and my arm got really tired.

But I didn't care if I was bad in bed. No. My career was bloating quicker than I was, I was the toast of fake-penis town, and I had a handsome woman. In this world, don't you just have to *look* like you're good in bed anyway? Of course.

So I lay back like a pillow queen and just let *her.* . . She fucked me in the car cruising through Golden Gate park; she fucked me in the bathroom of our favorite restaurant; she fucked me *going fifty miles an hour* around curves driving across some river I can't even remember the name of, in Yellowstone Park.

Life was good and I believed everything she said. She said *I love you, I love you, and you only; let's be monogamous for heaven's sake ... Let's stop using latex gloves!*

Stop using latex gloves? It'd gotten so that watching her clip her nails and snap on a glove was the Pavlovian sound of my dog food being opened up with a can opener, and wherever I was, I dropped to the floor and nipped at her ankles ...

But I never got into dental dams or Saran Wrap. Like hairy legs squashed under pantyhose, it just didn't do it for me, so I never even went down on her.

Without plastic I would give it a try. It was my turn to *pleasure her* so I said okay, okay, okay.

We got tested on Haight Street, where there was a women's health clinic on the second floor.

Hooter took a seat over by the big window, slouched down, and stared at all the posters about Pap smears, blood tests, and your baby's health.

I went to a bowl of condoms and started stuffing them into my pockets. To this day, if it's free I can't resist things. It doesn't matter if it's condoms, matches, or toothpicks. When I'm an old lady, it'll probably be handfuls of sugar packets. All my treasures end up getting thrown away with lots of lint, but I have that fantasy

0026-0

that one day I'll need to get out of a locked shed with only my quick wit, my condoms, toothpicks, matches, and mints. And it will have been worth everything. I'll laugh at everyone else locked in their sheds and I won't let anyone else out until I get tired of being alone.

I walked around the small waiting room and stood over a table with stacks of colored flyers on different sexually transmitted diseases. I picked up a sun-bleached green flyer on the dangers of syphilis and casually asked Hooter, "Okay, so this uh, means we're going to you know. . . ?"

She was looking at the ceiling. "See each other?" she filled in.

"Well," I said as I paced across the waiting-room floor waving a yellow flyer on gonorrhea, "we're already seeing each other, but are you sure we want to be you know, monogamous?"

"Yeah, I can do it."

"Are you sure? You know, you'd once had sex with everyone you've introduced me to in the last few months, so are you sure you can even be monogamous?"

"Yeah," she insisted. Her bouncing knee should've said something to me.

"Your knee's bouncing. Why's your knee bouncing?" I asked her.

"I'm just nervous about the blood thing, you know. I used to be a heroin addict."

"Oh, how interesting. A heroin addict. You mean like Sid and Nancy?"

"Yeah. That's why I wear a partial bridge."

"A partial bridge?"

"Yeah."

"Uh, what's a partial bridge?"

And she pulled the entire roof of her mouth out. That I still loved her after she put it back in was a testimony to my very mature and real love, and I wasn't even thirty yet.

"And how long are we supposed to be monogamous for?" I asked. "Are there like no breaks? No time-outs?"

"No, darling, I love you and we'll be together forever." She winked at me.

"Forever?" Forever stopped seeming like the next few months.

"I've been in a lot of relationships, and you get used to it."

"You mean you've had a lot of forevers? I'm not the only forever you've had?" And suddenly I was peeing on a tree and I wanted her cleaned out and only mine forever. No one could ever touch her, even if I didn't want to anymore. No one, I tell you, no one.

"Honey, I've had a lot of *nevers*. I've been with people I don't even remember. One night I was trying to pick up a bartender and she told me I'd already had her."

"Wow. That sucks. And you don't even remember. Well, okay, forever. But how are you supposed to remain monogamous with me? I'm not even that good at sex."

"Don't worry, you'll get better."

I walked around the room, read posters about leaving abusive husbands and listened to the buses outside for a few minutes. When that was no longer riveting, I picked up a mauve flyer on anal warts. "Wow. Anal warts. What a drag. Have you ever had anal sex?"

"Yeah, once. I was in my twenties and it was with a guy on a ship."

"You had sex with a guy on a ship?"

"Yeah, we were smuggling drugs into Florida."

"Smuggling drugs? Florida? "

"Yeah, and I got anal warts. It was months before I could have 'em looked at because once we were ashore, we had to hide."

"Hide?"

"Yeah, and then—"

"Wait—what about the anal warts? It says here they're really hard to get rid of," and I shrugged. "You know, just in case we decide to have anal sex."

"Oh, they got cut off. That was years ago. I'm fine now. But I'm not that into anal sex anymore."

"Yeah, I can imagine. Or I think I can. Well not really. I really must admit I have a huge admiration for women who can have anal sex. Anal sex with men. Whew, I bet you even Elizabeth Cady Stanton would've admired women who could pull that off."

Thinking more about it later on, I don't know if I still thought Elizabeth Cady Stanton actually had any free time to think about anal sex, or the people who pulled it off. But I had time, and still admired them. The same way I admired those who committed suicide off of bridges. I thought for a minute, put down the flyer and walked in front of the whitewashed fireplace filled with plastic bouquets of flowers. "I mean, how can you relax your anus that much? To me it's like if you can relax like that, you've reached a place of Zen. I'm far from there. Wow." I nodded. "You've actually had anal sex. You're not as dazed as you make yourself out to be, you know. You've got to be pretty smart to have anal sex. I think it's a waste to die without ever having had sex in every orifice you can." I started waving my fists in the air, walking in a small circle. "It's there! It should be used!—I just never could get past the pain. I'm missing out. I just know it." And knowing this just ate me up inside.

"Well," Hooter admitted, "yeah, but we'd taken a lot of drugs."

I sucked in my breath. "Really?" That depressed me a little since I never did drugs. I made bad enough decisions when I was straight. So I dropped into a chair by the window and watched the street below as a fat, legless lady in a motorized wheelchair pulled a guy in a manual wheelchair behind her. They zoomed away around the corner.

In what world would I ever be wild? Get thee to a nunnery.

Hooter started folding the anal wart flyer into a French blue airplane. "Oh yeah. At least I never got herpes. Cat had herpes."

"Cat? Who's Cat?"

"My last girlfriend."

"Your last girlfriend named 'Cat' had herpes?"

0-0031-0

"Oh yeah, but we were safe, darlin', so there's nothing to worry about." And she pushed the plane into the air.

"Uhm, okay, your last girlfriend had herpes." Her French blue anal plane hit me in the chest and dropped to the floor.

I exhaled as I picked up a flyer that was the color of swimming pools in Elvis movies. They must've sensed the lighthearted nature of the color, so they used it for crab information. Of course, AIDS got fire-engine red.

"Well, what's the penalty for cheating?"

"No penalty, darlin'. It's not hard when you love someone like I love you." Her knee kept bouncing like she was trying to bring out the butter in the situation.

"Well, of course there's got to be a penalty for cheating, or else there's no reason to be faithful. Like you get penalized for withdrawing money from pension funds early, so that's your incentive for keeping it there. That's what we need."

"Trust." Her knee bounced higher.

"Trust?"

"Yeah, trust."

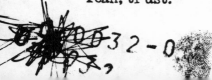

"I don't know about this trust thing. Trust is not enough. What if you cheat?"

"I won't cheat."

"Yeah, well, I'm not slick enough to cheat to make it equal if you cheat, so you'd better not cheat. If I'm gonna put my energy into this, I don't wanna be pushing this U-Haul truck load of love up the hill all by myself."

She looked at her watch and smacked her bouncing knees. "I sure wish they'd hurry up."

She picked up a *Woman's Day* magazine and I made a stack of all the flyers for myself to take home and read when I was more in the mood for terrifying myself and considering new obsessions for my repertoire.

I sat down next to her and read the same crack-baby poster she was staring at. Long after I had it memorized I said, "Well, we never came up with a penalty for cheating."

She laughed and patted my hand clutching the thick pile of colored disease flyers. "Darlin', no penalty. I love you and I never want to be with anyone else again."

"Never? Again?" And I thought about all the years ahead I was supposed to have with me, and suddenly I heard the snap of a tendon.

The sound of my brain going dead, and I rode the wave of Sapphic love and said, "Okay." And I stuck my pinky out for her to shake with her pinky and I said, "Cheat, and you die."

Laughing, she squeezed my pinky with hers and kissed my hand. "Okay, baby one."

"No, you don't get it," and I slid out of my chair and knelt down to her and pressed my arms over her bouncing knees and pushed them down hard. "I'm afraid I'm not kidding, love muffin, puddin' pie, sweet thing. Now you're more than just my Hooter with a View, my Sunday gal: cheat, and you *die*."

We got home and ceremoniously walked the box of latex gloves to the trash and she kissed me as sweet and long as the very first time, when she was too drunk to stand on her own.

In a husky voice, that almost made me laugh at my unoriginality, I said: *let's go upstairs.* And I would've tried to carry her, but she was almost a foot taller and besides, no one really carries anyone up a circular staircase unless they're trying to act out their own personal Ethan Frome and commit double suicide with their wife's cousin.

So we walked up like two people who wanted to live and have a couple of orgasms. The only ceremonial aspect of the moment was that I made her walk up first so my butt wouldn't be in her face.

I pulled off her jeans without words, so I'd seem to be the sexier one that way. And, anyway, it meant I didn't have the chance to say something stupid. I gently laid her back and parted her long French fries and just looked.

Ah, the big moment. It was time for lickin' carpets, shuckin' oysters, peelin' some peaches, and waxin' her floors for the very first time.

So there I was. Saying I was going to do it, *go ahead, go ahead, it won't bite you.* But there it was just sitting there, not moving and I wasn't too terribly sure about what to do, where to go, who to visit. *Tell me, tell me, tell me* I begged, before I have an art school/Cure-song flashback. Ay, it's too late. There is eyeliner everywhere. Somebody *please pass me my Gitanes.*

But it was really just all the pubic hair in my face.

Pubic hair wasn't a problem in my teeth or on any Coke can because she'd run her hand back and forth over herself real fast before I slid down between her legs. She knew what she was doing. But I could see that when she peed, she wiped with a lot of ferocity because I kept spitting out little balls of toilet paper on her thighs. At some point I fell off the bed, and like you do with horses, you get back on, especially if you're Catherine the Great.

And once I pulled everything back and *found the linen closet, I found the cash under the mattress, unearthed the liquor stash,* it was like going into a house I'd been in before.

Ah, euphemisms. I love euphemisms, even though the dirtiest word in the world is "euphemism," because it stands for *every* dirty word in the world.

Suck on that one.

Anyway, when her eyes rolled back in her head, *I knew the liquor stash was gone, the money was spent, and the linens were dirty. Yeeha! Bring on the dancin' girls.*

0-0037-0

Well, divin' for the ol' raisin got to be my favorite thing and I became a little raisin pig routin' around in her berry patch. I was glad of it too, since I sure as hell didn't have the finger-fucking thing down. So what if I was a one-trick pony? At least I could proudly show my face at any women's music festival, even though I'd rather be caught strung out and dead in a Porta Potti at some construction site. It's better to reject than be rejected.

Ah, diggin' for truffles got to be like sitting on Hooter's front porch drinking lemonade and smokin' a clove, and maybe I should've known something was awry when she started saying "stop it" everytime it happened when we were in her car or she was trying to watch some football game.

Oh, let me tell you children, hindsight is so Hubble telescope. Yes, Aunt Mad Dog knows of which she speaks, or however that saying goes. Now that I'm thirty, it's time for me to pass these things down.

She was about twenty years older than me, and her face was a little wrinkled from years of drinking hard and smoking long, but she was fine to me because she acted like a kid. In what now feels like only the first three days of our relationship, she'd wake up smiling, stretch herself out ten feet long and jump on top of my full bladder. She wasn't old. I felt old because I usually said no to morning sex because by the time I climbed down from my bed to go pee, I wasn't going back up.

But she learned to wake up first and bring me coffee in bed.

When someone brings you coffee, you can't say no. And if you do, you almost always deserve what happens after that.

We made Ramen noodles together and sat in the sun on weekends. When I stayed in the house making too many fake penises, she'd put me in her car and air me out.

But I think the real reason I loved her so much was that having her around in my house was like being alone, only better.

And like Mexican glass, there had to be a flaw, a crumb you can never quite gouge out of the surface./ A mosquito buzzing in your ear just when you're about to fall asleep: a couple of times a week she went away from me to drink until she passed out in the hallway, and some other things better left unsaid out of respect, especially with what ended up happening to her in the end.

Anyhow, I tried to understand. I tried to drink more. I tried to ignore it. And I tried to drink even more. I tried to just enjoy who she was when she was with me because she was the only one I'd ever been with who stuck around after admitting my thoughts about little girls in Catholic school uniforms going home, lifting up their green tartan plaid skirts, and bouncing up and down on their brothers' pointy laps while the *ABC Afterschool Specials* were playing in the background.

The only other person in my life who stuck around after hearing stuff like that was my sister, Glena Glane. But I never wanted to have sex with my sister, at least not yet, so Hooter was like two/two mints in one.

I learned real Zen from her about the same time I started calling her my little alcoholic. Not ambitious baby boomer Zen, about how to breathe deeply, eat wheat germ, and try to live forever while buying up San Francisco property and filling out order forms to have your head frozen. Real Zen. Hustler Zen. Painful alcoholic Zen, and I tried to leave her alone so I'd learn something.

So there we were wrapped together on the sofa, one of thousands of American couples watching *Matlock* on Monday nights right before it got canceled.

I wasn't going to club her with the 2x4, I just wanted to scare her.

I pushed the car door open, jumped out, thrust my arm straight out in front of me, and bent the nozzle on the top of the can. Reddi Wip spit all over her. She threw her arms up against it and that's when I dropped the can and clasped the handcuffs on her wrists. Still trying to cover her face, she screamed, and I pushed her down on her knees.

"Hey! Hey, what's going on!—Hey, weren't you her girlfr—?" A little man was walking toward us with a few Chihuahuas on some strings. The dogs were popping up and down like a kid's toy, barking with little hoarse yelps that I was sure would drive me crazy because Chihuahua barks are my kryptonite.

"Shut those goddamn rats up!" I screamed and a little vein in my forehead throbbed.

I held on to her with a fist in her wet hair which was slippery with gel and whipped cream and felt like a fistful of stringy pumpkin insides, and I waved the 2x4 at him and hissed, "Stay out of this unless you want your Chihuahuas to get it—this is our own private little Idaho!" And then I knew what the 2x4 was really for, so I threw it at the dogs.

The dogs became a hysterical blur, not unlike Hooter's knee that time in the women's clinic, and she started crying for help and he pulled the string of Chihuahuas to him and stood there agape as I pushed her into the back of the champagne Lexus 4x4. I jumped in behind her, slammed the door, and quickly tied an acrylic winter scarf over her eyes.

"Hey, where's the Bic lighter and ballpoint pen?" I asked myself out loud in a guttural voice that even scared me.

"Oh my God, why are you doing this?" She cried through snotty tears.

"Shut up!"

"What the hell are you going to do to me?"

While speeding away around corners, I reached over and messed through the glove compartment looking for the Bic lighter and ballpoint pen.

"Jesus Christ, what are you gonna do to me—?"

I pulled over and lifted her up by a fistful of slippery-pumpkin gray hair and licked whipped cream from her cheek and jammed the end of the scarf between her teeth and called "time-out" on the Quaker thing because paybacks are a bitch.

A bitch called Mad Dog.

Miss Mad Dog.

Everyone wants to know what happened, how it all started. Some of the papers had reported that I'd found a videotape or that I walked in on them in the middle of everything.

No, it wasn't as dramatic as all that. Not long after one of my art shows in New York, I got back after a couple of weeks and Hooter and I had pussy-mashing sex and the next morning I had crabs. Just like in one of those flyers from the clinic.

In the postwar Levittown between my legs, little crab families tried to tell me so many things about someone being unfaithful, but I crossed my legs and didn't want to listen. In tears, I went over to Hooter's apartment and asked her if the little crabs lied; she didn't know what I was talking about. Denied everything.

I sat at the kitchen table feeling embarrassed about being dramatic and loud, so I just changed the subject and asked what was on TV. Maybe I'd gotten it from a public toilet? But I always let it hang. Then what if crabs jumped up off the toilet seat? Could crabs jump? What did they *do* all day? I needed one of those flyers.

She pulled a pint of ice cream from the freezer, lit a cigarette, and unwrapped a Devil Girl candy bar and used it as a spoon.

Hooter loved those Devil Girl candy bars with the Robert Crumb cartoon drawings all over them. Thirty Devil Girl candy bars came in a pretty bright red cigar box with a big picture of Devil Girl all over it. She bought them by the case, so she had stacks and stacks of red Devil Girl boxes which she used to store weed, change, jewelry, dental dams, loose cigarettes, her collection of lighters, matches, shoelaces, notes, sunglasses, you name it. Devil Girl boxes were everywhere in her apartment.

"I don't know," Hooter said. "It's Monday, maybe *Matlock*'s on."

Matlock. She knew how to warm me from within in more ways than two. There's nothing warmer than escaping the inherited cynicism of my own bitter generation by cuddling in front of the TV under a blanket, watching Andy Griffith play a little ukulele and figure it all out, guest starring Don Knotts. Nothing warmer except for watching a two-part *Murder She Wrote* all in one night.

I sucked in my breath and asked, "Are you, could you be, uh sure? Is *Matlock* really on tonight?" I wanted MTV to be *Matlock* TV. All *Matlock*, all the time.

"Well, no, but I think so." And when she gently stabbed her Devil Girl chocolate into the ice cream, clenched her teeth, and scratched herself violently between the legs, I knew everything. It all clicked into place in reverse. And I knew I'd seen the other woman before. Once Hooter and I were having a beer at her favorite daily bar, the Mild Side West bar and grill, and a woman kept giving me dirty looks from the edge of the pool table. She didn't know me, and I didn't know why.

And before I even set Hooter's car on fire, I wanted to know the whole, ugly, inside-out truth. I refused to believe she was lying to me.

I said, I *have to go*.

And she said, what about *Matlock*?

I left in a whirlwind of tears and a new perfume called "Betrayal." *Stab, stab, stab* . . . The sounds of *stab, stab, stab* tickled my ears and I thought it might be a good idea to ignore them.

Instead, as I walked and scratched, I listened to the crabs, who had more honor than my lover, and they told me everything in one last-ditch effort to save themselves. The little crab people told me her name was Tule. It's pronounced like "tooly" and if this were a novel, I would've instantly shuddered in fear the instant I heard it. A tule fog is a heavy, dense fog that hugs the valley and causes hundred-car pileups.

And Tule Lake was once an American internment camp for *the Japanese*.

If I had known, maybe I would've moved 'to New York, lived in a basement, and forgotten about everything and started anew.

But I didn't.

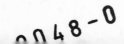0048-0

But I know now—with that Hubble telescope *hindsight*—I should've appreciated the horn-blaring significance of such a name.

Now, though, I'm thirty.

Tule was someone who would drink with Hooter until their livers tried to break out of their chest cavities and make a run for it. Tule thought passing out was the most adorable thing she'd ever seen. Tule was a brand-new divorcée with a couple of kids. Tule liked to drink, get high a lot, and dance naked for a few bucks at a bar in the Tenderloin District.

Oh, I didn't feel sorry for Tule. She was no lost soul, she was only slumming. Her grandmother had left her some kind of trust fund, but she wanted to dabble in the cheap side we all have.

We've all got a cheap side and we can't deny it. It's the impulsive, passionate, uneducated side of us that thinks "consequences" is just the back end of a '70s game show.

Since Tule was from Toledo, Ohio, it wasn't much of a trip for her to get back to a white trash state of mind. For her that meant hanging out with the leathery turkey basters and my girlfriend at the Mild Side West bar and grill.

I know from white trash. I've lived in both West Virginia and the Bronx. Those babes are all pretty much the same: thin eyebrows, bad skin, shiny clothing, plastic high heels, and an almost total disrespect for domestic animals. Pets and a personal life are luxuries you can't afford when you've been thrown off balconies yourself.

Stab . . .

I didn't like the crab friends I was ferrying around, but I did feel like I owed them a chance. I remembered back to a time when my house was infested with ants and someone came over in a Mexican accent and told me to spread cinnamon all over the house. That didn't work. Someone in a French accent told me to be gentle and put out a piece of bread with jelly on it, outside the back door and they'll leave my house and visit the bread.

So I started by sprinkling cinnamon between my legs and for a nice touch, I lit a candle and chanted "Go, go, go, my little crab friends. Follow the toast. . ." Anyway, that didn't work, so I sat naked on the kitchen floor in front of a piece of toast with jelly and told them to *go, go into the toast* until the phone rang.

"Hello?"

It was Hooter and she asked what was wrong.

"You lied to me, you, you, swampy flop!" I could only think of Elizabeth Taylor's violet eyes and friendship with Michael Jackson at a time like this. She was forever loyal to him. Stood by him even when he had little children sticking out of his underwear. Loyalty.

Something I knew nothing of. I burst into big afraid of Virginia Woolf tears.

I told her how I knew everything in detail, and in the end she finally slipped off the curb and admitted she'd been seeing Tule the Crab Woman for a long time, but that she really loved me, me, me. Why? Why? Why? And from there it all descended into songs where we already know the lyrics, so there is nothing more for me to say about how betrayed I felt. There is nothing for me to say about how I didn't understand. And there is truly nothing to say about how I was truly a bad lesbian in bed because there are no songs for clumsy lovers, even from the Ronettes.

But Hooter said no, I wasn't bad in bed. I was fine. Fine. High praise from a woman who could write a lesbian sex manual as long as she focused on technique instead of the usual holding hands and sharing feelings.

There's never been one like that. I know because I looked everywhere, and they don't even have pictures. Talk talk talk. Just like women to write a sex manual that's all about talking and holding hands and getting coffee for each other in bed. In the morning.

It was fine. Fine, fine, fine.

I wanted to tell her that she should've told me I was bad in bed. When she said I wasn't bad in bed, I knew she was lying. About everything. I hung up the phone.

This thing where you're supposed to make love to a woman brilliantly because you know what pleases her because you know what pleases you because you're a woman is bullshit. Absolute bullshit. Sometimes I could almost hear her say, "Well, yeah?" like she was waiting for me to do something better which only made the pressure worse. So I gave up and was content to be a pillow queen and get fucked until I cried for her to stop, please, please, I'm beggin' you please . . .

But when you're not doing your share, it's supposed to even out in the end somehow. I didn't want it to even out this way. Couldn't I have paid for dinner more often? Wait, I did! I lent her fifty thousand dollars when she wanted to expand the business and get more into s/m gear.

The first time she mentioned the idea, I scoffed at it. My face even looked like a scoff, whatever that is. I said, "s/m with chains, leather, and dog collars is wussy. Real, real, real s/m happens in poly/cotton blends and cheap pantyhose, when a woman gets the shit beat out of her and she goes back for more."

I can say whatever I want because it's a free country, and does one really need more than one or two friends, anyway? Not me. I'm getting used to the idea of growing old alone under a bridge with fifteen cats. But I digress because here's what the s/m people are like: "You're really missing out. It feels really good to stick needles in your nipples and exorcise all the shit your uncles did to you while your folks were out playing bridge."

I'm not sure how I'd feel if my sister later admitted to me that she likes getting wedgies during sex because I used to give them to her all the time. We used to fart in each other's faces, too, but that doesn't turn me on now that I'm older. Not yet, anyway.

It seemed like Hooter and me, we were the only couple not dragging each other around by dog collars and pumping fists and frozen ice cube trays up each other's butts.

You may be wondering if it hurts to be so uncool. Yes/sometimes/no. It makes me love *Matlock* and Andy Griffith even more and I pull my pants out of my butt and spit in MTV's face because when you're not cool, there's nowhere to fall, except off the sofa on a Saturday night like a little guinea pig.

And believing that I had nowhere to fall, I'd sat down with a sheer black scarf around my neck and written her a check for fifty thousand dollars. I was on my way back to New York to prepare for the last fake-penis show.

She said I didn't understand. I didn't. But I had faith in my true love darling. I wanted to be her darling back and say, if you build it, they will come, by signing over the check for fifty thousand bucks I made off of my fake penises. Like I said: they were doing well.

And if you're wearing sheer black scarves around your neck when you hand your alcoholic lover a check for fifty thousand, you almost always deserve what happens next.

GIRLS WHO ATE THE GIRL SCOUT COOKIES INSTEAD OF SELLING THEM.

My money! I ran over to the phone, nearly knocking over my dying spider plants which probably would've done better if I'd watered them with my menstrual blood, and dialed: auto 1. At that time she was number 1 in my memory. Now auto 1 is the number to my voice mail. When she picked up I said, where's my money, where's my money! She said sorry, it was all gone, and she hung up because what more can you say when you cheated on someone who gave you fifty thousand dollars and now it's all gone?

Nothing, except

Stab, stab, stab . . .

Stab, stab, stab . . .

Maybe try to get over the whole thing and fast before someone ends up with scissors sticking out of their eye sockets.

I sat, staring outside the window, getting in touch with the one feeling I'd paid so much money to learn how to recognize. Now my arms were feeling all trigger-happy.

And so

I threw the phone through my window, and then it dawned on me that now I didn't have a phone and now I didn't have a window.

0056-0

That's when I realized what was wrong with the Watts riots: if you're pissed, I mean, *really*, *really* pissed at someone, the idea is to let the mad dog shit on *their* lawn, not yours. I wanted to water my dying spider plants with *her* blood. I wanted to drain her like a little chicken.

Revenge makes you not care. Even if you're supposed to be a pacifist, the ferocious burn of energy is like a forest fire where Smokey the Bear is jumping up and down waving his arms, trying to get your attention, but you don't see him . . . and when you finally do, he resembles the lezzbian who once paw-fucked your girl and he's singing that old Frankie and Johnnie song about doin' his woman wrong.

Stab!

I turned and turned in a circle on my living room floor. Faster and faster until *Stab! Stab! Stab!* was loud, ripping static in my head. I turned and turned, faster and faster and finally, finally, I dropped to my knees while my apartment swayed like a great big ship off the coast of Argentina, a passionate country where husbands can get acquitted for murdering cheating wives, lovers, mistresses, and pool boys.

I jumped off board and swam through *well yeah, sures* in slow motion with wavering, high-pitched Martian music punctuated by whispers I couldn't quite make out: it was in the mail I opened, it was written in the curls of my hair, and it was in the sound of my toilet flushing. Every tampon I owned mocked me with row after row of well yeah, sures and each tampon cackled and cackled at me until I threw the box across the room and smashed their little tampon bodies against the wallpaper that had printed all over it, *Well yeah, sure.* And my Nena kitty didn't run out the door when I stepped on her tail, she hissssssed, *well yeah, sure.*

I ran to the back porch and bit into my lower lip to keep from bringing back up everything I'd ever eaten in my life, and I could taste the blood on the edge of my tongue. It tasted like homeless pennies and I had an awful lot of pennies coming back to me, pennies that she said she didn't have. Come to mama . . .

Stab, stab, stab

. . . Were those the little whispers I heard in my head?

Never mind. I wanted to hit her with a bag of pennies, that's what I wanted to do. But why hit when you could bludgeon? And why bludgeon when you could pulverize? Why pulverize when you could liquefy?

Stab! Stab! Stab!

What I needed was a big blender and a friend to help me come up with what's-red-and-white-and-in-a-blender jokes.

And all that I am about to confess here started innocently enough when I threw the toast away, and rode my motorcycle to the pharmacy with my coattails flying behind me. It was Hiroshima for the little crab people. Even the GI Bill couldn't help them now.

Stab ... Stab ... Stab ...

I knew I couldn't let her get away with it. I wanted to floss my teeth with Hooter's tendons. *Stab! Stab! Stab!* The voices yelled louder in my head until I poured lamp oil all over her dildoes and set them on fire.

It made the voices go away.

For a while.

COLLECTIVELY SNIFFING

Tuesday

OTHER PEOPLES' PANTIES

"THEY WERE ON THE URGE of BREAKING UP."
--- a guest on Jerry Springer

Jerry and Oprah.

You may watch both, but at some point you're going to have to make a choice.

In a time of unbridled sexual harassment lawsuits, chronic temporary employment, no health insurance, faux food and indigestible fat, bizarre beef industry problems, apathetic children who are whiny as hell and aren't gonna take it anymore until they get new cars, corporate general stores with creaky-wood-floor sound tracks, and mandatory cigarette, helmet, and seat belt laws, there is Oprah.

Once I wanted to be like Oprah. Yeah. I wanted to make the world a better place, lose a lot of weight, and convince people to clean all the change out of their sofas to send a bunch of kids to college.

Do you think Oprah has good sex with Steadman? Do you think that it's even important to them? I would say no, but every once in a while she talks in ebonics and it makes you think she could be a good nasty girl.

I tried to be cynical about Oprah, but I'm not made of stone. She got to me the same way Ralph Nader did. Only he's more of a panty warmer.

And you're going to buy an Oprah sweatshirt and you're going to believe her. Do you know why? Because your only other choice is to spend your day dialing 1-800 numbers just so you can be cruel to customer service representatives you'll never buy anything from, till you can turn on the tube and watch Jerry Springer with a clear conscience.

Jerry Springer was born with an eyebrow raised. With Jerry, there is no center, nothing can hold, the world's going to hell in an Easter basket because even the bunny laces the eggs with razor blades.

With Jerry, you get lighter furniture because it's gonna get thrown around. All ye be forewarned: his is not a show for Quakers.

I tried to watch Oprah. A show for Quakers. I tried to make a nourishing Oprah meatloaf for myself, drop a little lavender on my pillow slips, play a little Chopin and feel the warmth of self-love spread throughout my body. Instead, the warmth of my self-love made bloody ground beef sculptures that looked like Hooter's neck and strangled them like Play-Doh and stabbed them with spoons.

I wrote Oprah letters asking for help to keep me from doing something very, very bad, but I got form letters back telling me to stay away. That they'd extracted my fingerprints from my notepaper and that if I showed up in Chicago, I'd be escorted "back" to Jerry Springer's studio.

"Back"?

Maybe Jerry would have a bitter, lonely home for me. Fine. Then it would be Jerry.

I wrote Jerry a letter and got a form letter back. A letter that had been so overly Xeroxed it was nearly sideways and covered with big black dots like those tasteless jokes that got copied and faxed around offices before all the sexual harassment suits—but this time with two tickets and a promise of airfare and accommodations if I could convince the "other party" to make an appearance on the show. The letter ended with a filled-in Xeroxed signature of the show's producer, followed by an 800 number.

The ink was so filled in, I spent the next hour making sure I could tell the difference between a "3," "8," "9," and "4" so I could turn to Jerry Springer for solace.

Solace from a man who throws hired baby kittens smeared in chicken blood at pit bulls and encourages us all to embrace just a little bit of our anger and sense of injustice. Jerry Springer encourages us to get in touch with the skittish and cornered animal nature we have in all of us. Whether we're black, yellow, red, or American blue we can all be proud white trash on parade.

Afraid of that big black man carrying the baseball bat with the neat little scar over his frontal lobe, demanding his money back? No fucking way, man! Afraid of that Ku Klux Klansman with his hood on backwards and a runaway chainsaw in his hand?
No fucking way, man!

The day is young and the chairs are light, but the Pepsi's not.

Make no mistake; Jerry's an artist. Every day he's thinking of new ways to make his chairs lighter and easier to swing. When they can fly around like popcorn, the ratings go up. They must be light enough for a pregnant mother of three, living in the projects on sugar fumes, to lift the chair up and swing it at the cheatin' father of the baby in her womb and tell him none of the children are his. And yet the chairs must also stand the test of time and not look like the ones in the food stamp office.

I dialed the 800 number and my future would've been a personalized Triptik straight to a very embarrassing and public hell if all the numeric variations I tried hadn't been wrong. Wrong, like this is not the way to deal with anger. If I'd been in a more spiritually open place like I am now that I'm thirty, I wouldn't have painted myself into such a dumpy little corner. I would've seen it as a sign, a gentle red brick of love being hurled at me from the heavens.

Thirty has brought with it all kinds of green, rolling fields of promise. I do dishes within mere days of dirtying them, and don't pick my clothes off the floor and smell them nearly as much as I used to.

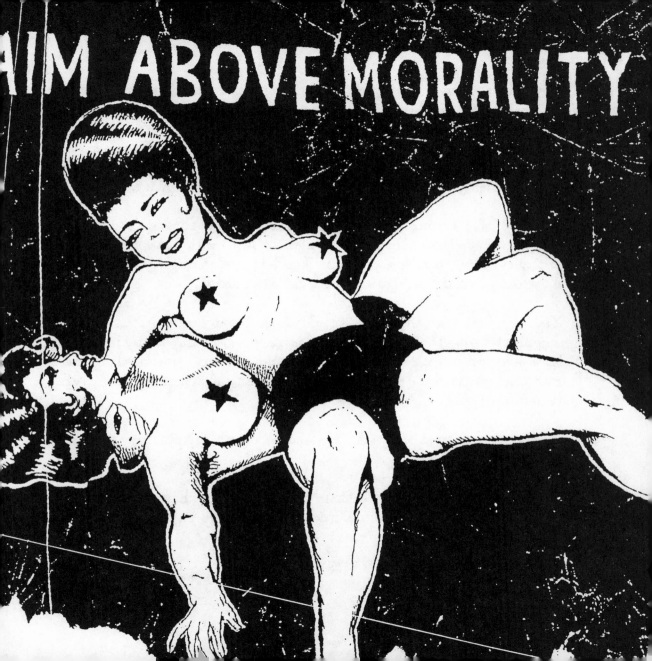

I want to warn any of you who will try this at home, that revenge is lonely and slippery like an avalanche where you only have a small air pocket in which to smoke cigarettes, re-inhale your own secondhand smoke over and over again. And since your friends will think you're insane, you'll be alone, very alone, disinfecting your wounds with your own urine like they did in the eighties.

Leaving a burning bag of dog shit outside someone's door and ringing the bell so they have to step in it to put out the fire, will probably lead to worse things. The kind of things you wouldn't show photos of or tell your grandchildren about.

Yep, it's just like they said in all those scratched-up filmstrips in school: stealing that first pack of gum or smoking that first joint, tiny acts of revenge lead to something bigger like stealing cars, running your own drug cartel, or becoming a crack ho' and giving two-dollar head.

Better you should play it safe and become a temporary secretary without benefits.

But like many of you former Sid and Nancy heroin addicts out there, I didn't care, either. I knew I could stop any time I wanted. Any time, baby doll.

When Hooter wasn't at home, I assumed she was over at Tule's apartment. I asked around and found it was supposed to be a canary yellow-bellied house two blocks away. So I went and I threw eggs at the windows, rang the bell, and ran in my own special little slow motion D-cup kind of way.

See? Kid stuff. Kind of cute and ironic, even, running away from a yellow house and all. Makes you want to pinch my cheek and give me a Popsicle, eh? Well, not so fast. You'd better put down the ducky.

I didn't get into trouble however until I started burning lingerie-clad effigies in front of the apartment.

I'd hung up the effigies on a little tree in front of the apartment with big knitting needles stuck through notes over their body parts that said, WELL YEAH, SURE! WELL YEAH, SURE! WELL YEAH, SURE! pinned to them.

But it was taking a while for the straw to ignite, so I was still there trying to work that damn childproof lighter, when the door opened and out came a rush of warmth and a smell of newspaper and forgotten mangoes. The old lady smell. I whipped around, and an old woman had opened the door of the apartment to take out a small kitchen bag of trash.

In the background I saw Hummel figurines on her television set and I realized it was the wrong house. When she saw what I was doing, she threw her trash at me and spit something in German. She hobbled to the phone and I left to double-check Tule's real address in a phone booth.

I felt embarrassed and sorry for the old lady for an hour or two, and then I figured it might not have really been a mistake. Maybe she needed to find out what it felt like to be Jewish in 1939.

That's probably what Shirley MacLaine might've said, because according to Shirley, there are no mistakes: we all get flat tires for reasons.

I started feeling alone. My friends stood next to me as I put sugar in Hooter's gas tank, slashed her tires, cut more of our dildoes up and superglued them to her front door. They stood there trying to put out the fires and told me that I was scaring them. Really scaring them, but I didn't listen.

I told them not to worry, this was just something I had to get out of my system. A little hate phase. I told them to give hate a chance because hate can be cute like Charles Manson in love, walking through a New York rain in Washington Square, arm in arm with the one he loves, passing Woody Allen and Soon-Yi, who are holding hands under an umbrella, looking at Polaroid snapshots of her pubic racing stripes.

PANTING LIKE A LITTLE CHICKEN
RAMPANT CHAFING... HOW COME WE NEVER HEAR MORE ABOUT IT?

"So what did she do after she got the chicken from the grocery store?" I was asking my one last friend, Mary, for actual revenge stories for more ideas.

"Then she nailed it above the doorway and let the juices drip into a pan on the floor."

"Why did she put a pan on the floor?"

"To catch all the blood so it wouldn't make a mess."

"Why didn't she just let them run onto the floor if she was so mad at him?"

Mary said there is a funny kind of love in revenge, especially when you don't want to get blood on their floor.

Well, the draining chicken idea wouldn't work because I couldn't get in her house. I'd already taped her key to a telephone pole on a piece of paper with her address on it.

I was dry. I needed some help. From a professional.

See, I tend to black out when it comes to differentiating between minutes and years, but sometime like a year earlier, I'd decided to start my own motorcycle gang, T h e F l a m i n g I g u a n a s.

Everyone shuddered in appropriate fear when they heard the name. A week later I learned how to ride a motorcycle around the block. It was such a conceptual kind of motorcycle gang, especially in its early renegade days before I could even purchase liability insurance. And of course, now that I'm thirty, I have the maximum in motorcycle insurance.

Since it was a wildly conceptual postmodern kind of gang, I was its sole member and the gang leader. I was fine with this because I didn't want anyone following me around and I didn't want to follow anyone else around, either. But even still, I found myself so threatening, sometimes I feared me, and under threat of jamming my own head down a toilet and flushing again and again until I finally gave in, I'd make myself do all sorts of crazy things like add too many quarts of oil to my bike and wait to see what happened.

It wasn't long after I took off in search of pretentious answers from America, that I came across a couple of people in Texas who had a trailer bed and breakfast. The man also ran a stalking/revenge business. His name was Bark. Bark Flammers and his number was 1-800-REVENGE, PUNISH, or 800-SLAWTER. I don't remember now whether one or all three worked, but I think I got lucky on the first one. If you want to call, he's not doing that kind of stuff anymore. Not after everything that went down.

Went down. Like that? When you start getting bad, really, really bad, you start talking in slang. Maybe it'll be old slang from the forties, but who the hell cares. It's kind of like being really, really good, going to church and talking in tongues. Except you're being baaad.

I asked Bark Flammers if he'd be willing to take a trip out to San Francisco so I could hire him as my revenge campaign manager. I think that what convinced him was that if lesbianism was chic, then lesbian *revenge* was sure to be even more chic. Cooler than being accepted into Studio 54 for a night of unwrinkled polyester debauchery.

Lesbian revenge was nothing like heterosexual revenge, which *always*, *always*, *always* looks like white-trash-on-a-talk-show no matter what color you are or how expensive your clothes are.

Bark Flammers said sure, that he had a hundred and one revenge ideas on his laptop. He said he was writing a book, like a Betty Crocker type cookbook of revenge ideas and he wanted to get it published and go on talk shows. We did a little consultation where he asked what I'd already done and what I hoped to accomplish. I said, more. He said I needed a goal. A goal? Yes, revenge needed to have a purpose.

"A purpose?" I asked.

"Yeah, a purpose."

"Well, like I want to get her back. Make her suffer."

"Well, how far do you want to go?"

"All the way."

"Well . . . It's only fair to let you know I've really got a lot of ideas."

"No, no, no. You don't understand. I've already left episodes of *Gilligan's Island* on her answering machine. I've already faxed her a loop of paper so she runs out of fax paper. I've already slashed her tires, put sugar in her gas tank . . . But I don't feel better. I want to go all the way, do the big bang."

"The big bang?"

"Yeah."

"Well, okay. We'll talk about the details of 'how' when you get a clearer idea."

"Good. I can wait until you get out here. I need to really give this some thought."

He said that was fine because he needed a couple of weeks to get everything ready so he could leave for a while.

See, Bark also shared a trailer-home bed-and-breakfast business with a French fagette he married so she could stay in the country.

Her name was Kris Kovique and she'd had a bad year because she had to get one of her tits cut because of breast cancer. She told Bark Flammers that she'd save it and make a little change purse for him. But they wouldn't let her. Imagine that. Another example of how a woman should have a right not only to control her own body, but a right to her own body *parts*.

Afterwards in the hospital, she said she looked like a spayed cat. Bark tried to make her feel better by telling her not to feel so bad because his mother had run off with his foreskin. But as you can imagine it didn't assuage her pain since Kris said that, unlike her, he was too young to remember anything.

Whoa, horsie! *That* was a mistake she'll never make again. You would've thought that she said something about his mama and spit on his feet at the same time, because the blood ran to Bark's face and his voice started shaking like a hula girl. Bark said that unconsensual circumcision was the reason for all of his internal and outward loneliness and bitterness. Because he's lost penile and emotional sensitivity and it all comes down to that missing flap. And he's not alone. No siree.

Kris had gauze bandages and rubber drains coming out of her chest and she asked Bark to ring for the nurse because she was in a lot of pain and a little nauseous from the anesthesia.

"Sure," Bark answered, "you may be in pain, but what about millions of infant boys getting circumcised *without* anesthesia?"

"Then if that's true, how come they can't do heart surgery the same way?" Kris groggily asked.

Bark ignored her and pressed on, "Look, I've been feeling ripped off ever since my genital mutilation."

"You're buggin' me."

"Imagine what the elephant man would've felt if he found out he'd been born *normal* and this—" Bark unzipped his fly and pulled down the front of his boxer shorts and pointed to himself "*this*—is what they'd done to him. I am an amputee and I'll always wonder where is the rest of me."

Kris squinted her eyes shut and turned her head, "Okay, okay—your mother sold your foreskin at a Bavarian meat market, now leave me alone."

"There you go. Making fun of me at inappropriate moments. It's people like you who don't want to hear about factory-farmed chicken so they can eat their meat in peace."

Still looking away from him, she replied, "Speaking of eating meat in peace, do you honestly think *chicharrón* is always fried *pork* skin? Remember the fried pork skin shortage of '58?"

"Oh no . . . No . . . That can't be right, it's disgusting."

"Yes, fried pork skin is disgusting, and so are penises." Kris turned back at him, cringing. "I still think they all look like amputee stumps no matter how you slice them."

"See! See!" He poked at her chest. "That's because rampant circumcision *deforms* men."

"No, Bark, it's because I'm a *real* lesbian. Not one of those pretend ones who just wants to piss off her boyfriend for a little while. I've never even touched one."

"A pretend lesbian or a penis?"

"A penis, of course. Would you please hand me the water pitcher? My mouth is dry."

He put the water pitcher on her stomach and softened his tone. "That's another thing we've got in common, my friend. I'd been brought up to never touch another man's penis, either. To be ashamed in comparing so I wouldn't be angry at my mutilation. At first I was envious of uncut men. I even envied my dog. In grade school, I developed foreskin revenge fantasies that startled the other children. Some of the nuns told my parents it was an obsession, but they were wrong. Whenever I take a shower now, I ease the bitterness by retracting my own pretend foreskin."

Covering her ears, Kris yelled, "Bark. Too much. Wrong way—ding, ding, ding—change the subject or go away. Do you think you're bugging me? Hmm. *Looks* like you're bugging me, *feels* like you're bugging me. You must be—"

"—Did you know that foreskin means frenulum?" Bark was staring past her, shaking his finger, trying to make a profound point to her as much as himself, "And frenulum means—now get this—*little friend.*"

"Look, you're lucky we don't cut the entire dick off, you sniveling swine."

Bark hung his head and looked down at his own little mole rat just dangling there. "I was circumcised when I was eight days old," he sniffled, "I can still remember it like it was yesterday. I didn't want it and was unable to stop it because I couldn't even hold my head up yet." Bark wiped a little tear from his eye, swallowed the drama, and looked back at Kris. "I haven't been the same since."

She covered her eyes, "Good. Now, would you *please* ring for the nurse?"

"When I was a kid, I prayed I'd get my foreskin back in heaven. Living in a world without foreskin. It's a separation of ourselves from nature by the tyranny of the circumcisors. The oppressors want us to mull through sex lives not knowing all the sensitivity we're missing. Did you know all the horror started in the 1800s to discourage masturbation?"

"Can you at least pour some water for me? I can't move this arm and hold the cup at the same time."

He lifted the pitcher from her stomach, poured water into a cup and handed it to her, "No, you don't understand! Gone forever is my foreskin's millions of cells, fifty nerve endings, a hundred sweat glands, and several thousand feet of blood vessels. Gone forever is my penis's own form of natural personal lubrication! But not to worry. All may not be lost. Foreskin reconstruction techniques really can help me regain lost sense of wholeness and moistness—"

"—smegma."

"Excuse me?"

"You want to regain your lost *smegma*. Would you please ring for the nurse?"

"The genital mutilation industry brainwashes parents to do it so that boys will look just like dad and other boys."

"Not so they'll look like mom and other girls?"

"We all have to breaking the silence healing the patriarchal wound."

"Heal the patriarchal worm?"

"*Wound.* Heal the patriarchal *wound.* One day I'll show you. Oh yes, you mock me now, but you know, I was at a national men's gathering before you and I got married, and a man got up, played his guitar and sang what we simply call, 'The Foreskin Song.' "

"You've *got* to be kidding," she gasped like a lesbian out of water. "Look, could you please push that red button? I *really* do need the nurse."

Kris wasn't kidding because she fought like a real trooper to control those retching spasms. And Bark wasn't kidding either, because he started to sing a little foreskin ditty by a real man named Jeff Grant.

Kris screamed for the nurse call button. As Bark sang on, she painfully tried to push her body to the edge of the hospital bed and reach for the cord to the nurse button, "Now just hand me that little box. I beg of you . . . just wedge the red button under my chin."

"But wait, you haven't heard the end of the song. It ends on a climax of hope because he has a son . . . "

In time, things eventually ended on a climax of hope for Kris, because not long after, she fell to the floor screaming in agony and landing on a stainless steel bedpan. Lucky for Kris, it was empty. And once the nurses burst into the room and noticed Bark standing there holding a small bouquet of flowers and his penis dangling over the elastic of his boxer shorts, they firmly asked him to leave, which he quietly did, escorted by orderlies, because the looks on the nurses' faces reminded him of those nuns. Bitter, lonely nuns from oh so many years ago.

Later, Flammers lost steam once he learned that foreskin restoration takes two to four years of constant stretching (the same amount of time it takes to get a postgraduate degree) and the aesthetic reality is that a homemade foreskin is flabby and creepy, so he decided to make do with the decreased sense of pleasure that comes from the rampant chafing of an exposed glans against the inside of a pair of jeans.

Afterwards, Kris went through chemotherapy, and when she wasn't dry heaving, she was reading aloud to Bark from an anthology of death. It was a stapled-together book, appropriately covered in the blood of paper cuts. Different chapters focused on different ways of dying, including what physically happens to you when you're hanged or electrocuted.

Understandably, Bark found this depressing, so once she no longer needed his help, he thought it might be time for a little getaway.

Kris was glad for the time alone and with Bark gone, it opened her up to a relationship with a little rabid feminist chippy named Bootsy. Bootsy was a little blond number, pretty like a sequined dress on sale in the mall, with a nose that could cut a diamond. She was the kind of pillow-queen feminist who didn't want to pay her own rent. You know the kind. The kind who—"uh oh!"—only has

75 cents when the pizza comes. Enough about her, though. Let me take a moment to explain just why I talk about lesbians like I do when, even now, I've only known three women in the biblical sense.

Well, let me just say that here on out that I can say whatever I want about lezzbians because I am the child of *Our Bodies Ourselves* and I've paid the lesbian dues far into my next life. I don't have to rest my hand on another girl's knee ever again to know why the caged bird sings. For instance, lesbians may not be as wacky as your average zany, mad cap gay man, but that doesn't mean lesbians need less love. It's a complicated thing, because you can't just simply *love* a lesbian. It requires a little more work, like adding sugar to your coffee. Unlike hanging out with needy, insecure straight girls who expect you to read their minds, or morose, rock-star cartoonists who expect you to care, or straight boys who just want you to shut up and suck their dicks—all of whom can inspire you to break your beer glass and slit your wrists with the shards—Rea Lesbians can be so cool to hang around, because between all the real tits on the pool table, deep voices, soap operatic love lives, and karate kicks, it's well worth it because they're not worried about getting crow's-feet when they laugh.

Unless they're from L.A./Or unless they're new lesbians. The gung ho ones who buy all the rainbow keychains and instigate cock fights with their grandfathers over the phone on Christmas.

And another thing, Rea Lesbians don't really like the word "lesbian." I've learned it's not just my mom and her girlfriend.

A lot of lesbians think it sounds like something halfway between dinner and a condition.

And "lesbianic" sounds like what happens after a lesbian stops doing lesbian things, when all her parts wear out and she's wearing muffpés.

So the bottom line is that the word "gay" is better because it actually sounds more like fun. "Probably won't be," my friend Cherry Mary once told me, "but *could* be."

When I was in grade school, I went through radical feminism and man-hating in the seventies along with my mom and her raped friends. I remember it all. I may not have been alive to remember where I was when JFK got shot, or when Jayne Mansfield married Mr. Universe, but I'm thirty. Long past the point of "young lady" and well into the land of "ma'am." However, I do remember where I was when I heard there was going to be a *Bionic Woman* TV show, and that's got to count for something in this high-rent world.

I picketed *The Story of O* at nine, and by ten I sat with a huge mirror propped up between my legs and broke my hymen in front of menstrual-blood-tasting lezzbians handing me tiny tampons covered in Vaseline. Even though it was a miniature tampon no bigger than the business end of a house key, the kind I could now easily shoot across the room if I sneezed, back then it was huge and I cried like I was trying to stick a yule log inside me. Now I fondly remember that it looked like an emaciated albino mouse from England's shiny vinyl Mod Years.

They didn't want me to grow up fearing my body as they'd grown up to fear theirs. Instead, I grew up to fear white boys in pickup trucks named "Bubba" and lesbians who talk about their feelings.

They passed around that big gallon of cheap, sweet wine to each other and held shadeless lamps over me so I could see. We bonded in that special way, and intuitively sensing my vaginal panic, they coached me to relax and told me their stories of how it was better now. In their day they had to wear belts and pins and their moms never told them anything about menstruating, so they thought they were bleeding to death for leaving the milk out.

So being the recipient of simple modernity, in solidarity for my feminist mothers, I gritted my teeth and pushed until I felt a "pop!" and screamed like Tarzan getting a surprise cavity search with a very big green banana.

I realized intercourse would be like trying to poke a penis through a paper cut and I decided never to let any man stick anything inside me unless he was way, way smaller than the cap on a ballpoint pen.

I look back and laugh, as I've ended up with a stretched-out throat and a great whistling cavern between my legs.

On a quiet night, if I cross my legs, I sound like a cat smacking up some cold cuts, and I have to close my throat by wrapping my hands around my neck and squeezing. That's what'll happen to a girl who ran away from her dad and traded her math book for *Cosmopolitan* articles on the Eastern way of love and made Linda Lovelace's throat something to compete with instead of looking up Stagecoach Mary or Sojourner Truth.

I didn't actually get my period until two years later when I was twelve, had run away and was temporarily living with my friend Gloria at her prostitute-mom's house. Gloria was the prettiest thing in the world because she was half black and Mexican, and she could do the nastiest and sexiest things with tube tops. She was my first real mentor.

Gloria taught me to lay on my back in the tub and spread my legs under a gushing water spout. She taught me how to flirt so you get things like gas for free, but hold back just enough so you don't actually have to have sex with them even if you don't get the green stamps. It's a fine art of putting out just enough and holding back just so. This is why I can smell the conniving plans of a Bootsy five miles away. Girls like this don't fall in love; they take prisoners.

That skill ended up coming in handy when I ran away a lot, because men will do things for you, but if you acted too uptight, they'd want to take you and make you do things. But if you played loose, like you just weren't up to it, they didn't bother you. It's hard to explain, but I think pure innocence is sexy to some guy who buys you a couple of milk shakes at the bus station while nasty innocence maybe makes him think twice. Like you might be more trouble than you're worth. Maybe, just maybe, I'm full of shit, but all I know is I made it out of my stretchy-throated adolescence alive, without even a crab.

Anyway, since it was two weeks before Bark Flammers would arrive, I kept myself busy by preparing his room in my apartment.

Bark and I were born on the same day and as far as we're concerned, August tenth should be a national holiday. People should take off work, drive around eating and smoking while talking about having sex with the pedestrians at stoplights.

And because of this astrological connection, we have a kind of an astral shorthand with each other. For example we both think that you can do something really bad to someone and still be a good person. Just don't cross the path with us in it. You should've seen the sign. It's up there. Right *there*.

But that's all just deep, "a friend is . . . " stuff. Don't get too choked up, though. Where we really clicked was with our love for porn. We watched it the way other people watch *Good Morning America*. And since we were both bisexual, we could share, which really cuts down on costs if you stop to do the math.

That doesn't mean we sat around with our hands in our laps. We usually went away to our separate rooms and didn't really watch porn together unless we were eating supper. Then it was just like background music.

So on this particular night, I picked up a porn movie and some Vietnamese food. So much fresher than Chinese. I got a bisexual movie where the guys wore strap-ons with two-foot-long penises that looked like atrophied third legs just hanging there. They were trying to pass them off as real, so the guys who wore them wore shorts so we wouldn't see the straps. The whole thing was pretty gross, and they could even make the fake penises spooge. I loved that word, and still do even now that I'm thirty. Bark said "spooging" sounded like an Olympic sport.

I was preoccupied with trying to figure out how they made it work, but they were a little too clever for me with the camera angles, even though when they bent over we could see their real penises poke out from tucking them back up against their *perineum*. That wasn't real attractive, to say the least.

So there we were: Bark was eating crab. He was barely watching because he didn't really like to watch porn and eat, but nothing good was on TV. When one guy did the fake spooging thing on another guy's back, I asked Bark if it was real because a whole lot of stuff came out, and I didn't remember how much really came out of a guy.

Bark looked up just as he was sucking in a crab leg while the guy squirted and it almost made him vomit, so we turned the video off.

He was becoming a good friend, and I almost forgot the purpose of his being there until he threw his trash away and asked if I realized what purpose I had in revenge. I told him I didn't have one yet. So I said I'd think about it some more.

That night he went out to the kind of sauna where married men went to give blow jobs and I stayed in to come up with some new fake-penis ideas in front of the TV.

A show came on about all these guys in prison, and there was this
one big guy who made the little guy on the bottom bunk his lady, his
woman, his punk. And to prove to the little guy that he owned him,
he sat on the back of the little whimpering one's legs and held the
flame of a lighter underneath a ballpoint pen so he could carve and
burn the tattoo of a swastika into his tense butt cheek.

Lions and tigers and bears, oh my . . .

It was so, so perfect, I shuddered.

DEVILGIRL

In the morning I wrote a note to Bark on the back of Hooter's restraining order, saying that I was borrowing his car and would bring it back later.

At the time, I fancied that revenge made me think so sharp and clear, I felt my eyes naturally squint all the time because I no longer focused; I scanned. Nothing makes you as stupid as love and as intelligent as revenge. My teeth felt like warm steel, my blood cut its way through my sugarcane veins like machetes and I felt powerful like when I was a kid and bending a boy's arm behind his back was as easy as folding a green twig.

And all this was before 6 A.M.

I covered the windows of Bark's Lexus 4x4 with taped-up gay newspapers and covered the back with a padded moving blanket. Next, I filled a small brown lunch bag with a Bic lighter and a ballpoint pen. At the corner store, I got a clothesline and bought up all the canned Reddi Wip they had, which was about nine cans. Those I put on the seat next to me.

Next, I rolled quietly onto one end of her street, pulled a ski mask over my head and just sat there patiently. It was a classically foggy San Francisco morning and the block was quiet even though there was a crack house in the middle up for sale at a quarter of a million dollars. And from there it would only bid upwards. Clock radios were just going off with mariachi music, and I waited at

the corner, keeping the car at a steady idle, waiting for Hooter to come out.

But what if she slept at Tule's? No. She didn't like sleeping with mothers who had children barging in the bedroom.

I thought of sleeping with a woman who had children and I felt too young. It seemed too creepy and Freudian. I was embarrassed that I had such a perverted Elvis side to me. For some reason Elvis didn't want to sleep with Priscilla after she was a mom. I thought, bad man! Bad man! when I heard it, but now I think I might understand. It'd be like having sex with a teacher, and there are just some boundaries I'm not prepared to cross. Maybe that's why I'm so bad in bed, because good sex is all about crossing boundaries and trying not to use that one "safe" word that'll put an end to it all. Hell, just to be safe, I pepper my small talk with "safe" words because you never know.

I felt shame at that moment. Not for what I was about to do, which might've been helpful in averting the train wreck that was becoming my life, but because I was preoccupied with feeling shame about identifying with Elvis's creepier side.

And then I thought about what I was about to pull off, and I felt pride. This was going to be the finale. Bark could stay here if he wanted, but I had to do this alone. Couldn't drag anyone else into this.

I waited a good two hours, idling patiently and wasting Bark's gas, before I lifted the bottom of the damp mask to the top of my lip and lit a cigarette, and there she was at the other end of the block, unlocking her car door at a perfect and unaware 9:15 in the morning.

Have I already welcomed you to Argentina?

0-0092-0

STUPID URBAN
BUNGIE JUMPING

Basically, once I handcuffed her and pushed her into the back of the car, I wound the clothesline around her ankles and slipped her a mickey like I was jamming medicine in my cat's mouth. I drove around a few blocks so the Chihuahua man couldn't find us in case he wanted trouble.

Until she passed out, I kept giving her whip-its. I tore a tiny hole in the bottom of the bag with my teeth, reached over to the backseat, pulled the scarf down covering her mouth, and held the paper bag over her mouth and nose. I barely touched her nose but it started to bleed a little anyway. All her nose parts were pretty fragile because she'd also been a coke addict during the disco years.

But it wasn't messy. I just wiped the blood off the end of her nose with the tip of my finger, then smeared it on the seat. She seemed to stop bleeding, so I kept sticking Reddi Wip nozzles into the bottom of the bag so she was breathing the nitrous oxide. Asleep, she was giggling uncontrollably. I leaned against the front seat and looked down at her with something like regret, love, and fury. Oh, my little Hooter, she loved altered states of consciousness.

For her, pharmaceutical Latin was as good as dirty pillow talk.

I didn't know where I could take her. I'd know when we got there. I wasn't even sure if I could go through with this now that she was at my mercy. I was raised Quaker by two liberals who were still trying to save the world. I was heading south, both literally and figuratively.

And this is why the historical pendulum swings and history's got to repeat itself. Old people got their heads bashed in fighting for a forty-hour work week, old people got ripped apart by dogs so their kids would be able to vote, and us snot-nosed kids got it so easy, we complain there's no one to bother voting for and we say unions are a major pain in the ass.

Would I keep going, or would I stop? Literally and figuratively. I was literally planning on stopping anywhere, somewhere in that netherworld between L.A. and San Francisco. It's like the *perineum* because it t'aint neither here nor there.

Figuratively, I didn't know about stopping. I don't know if I can explain, but it was the kind of thing I wanted to go through because I wasn't sure if I'd regret not doing it when I got old and was in a convalescent home with my legs cut off or something. Maybe I should've channeled this energy into something more productive, found something more beneficial to sink my teeth into and fight for, like the rain forests. But I didn't think I could stand being in the company of white people so liberal you can *feel* their guilt. The kind who pronounce "Guatemala" better than the Guatemalans.

I had to grab the brass ring, no matter how hot red or evil. There are so many movies where you see old people raising their canes and wheeling around the rest home shouting something like, "Damnit, I wish I'd done blah blah blah back in 1947 when I didn't have this damn colostomy bag."

I wasn't sure, but I didn't want to take any chances. I wanted to go all the way, short of death. I didn't really have the urge to kill, because it didn't seem like a good idea to kill Hooter for revenge because she wouldn't have a chance to suffer. Suffer. Suffer. I knew things were teetering on the edge of legal, but when you're getting in touch with your raging bitter and unpredictable side, legal is like one of those Spanish words I couldn't understand because it had nothing to do with me picking something up at the store for my grandma.

After four hours of driving, I found the perfect spot. It was a little dead end where I could nestle the car among the craggy brush along the coast.

I looked in the back. Hooter was sleeping like a baby. Like a long, skinny baby who snores a little bit and leaves its eyes open just a little sliver so you can see the whites.

Again, I reached over the front seat, and rolled her over onto her stomach. Then I pulled her jeans down and when I saw her miniature butt that I could cover with one hand, I didn't know if I could actually do it.

I sat back down and looked out at the ocean through the windshield. You're supposed to get all the answers to everything when you look at the ocean, so I rolled a cigarette to officially think this over.

Again, another chance to think might've saved me from all the trouble that was to come, but no: a knock at my window and I dropped the cigarette into my crotch and I screamed.

I was looking right smack at a copper. They call 'em California Highway Patrol, and I hear the training's so rigorous, it's hard not to stutter and sweat as a sign of respect and contempt.

I pulled the burning cigarette from underneath me and noticed the ember was gone. I smiled at him, pushed the car door open, and jumped out. He put his hand on his gun and stepped back.

"No, no, no," I said waving my arms in the air, "you just scared the, uh, bejeebies out of me and I dropped my cigarette."

"Please step away from the car, ma'am."

"Yeah, yeah, sure."

He reached forward and pulled the cigarette from my hand and smelled it. Then he threw it on the ground.

"License and registration, please, ma'am."

I noticed his police-issue black and shiny motorcycle boots, all the way up to his knees and I felt an uncomfortable stirring that seemed so predictably girlie. Predictable in a historical romance novel kind of way that would've made Gloria Steinem and Kate

Millett wince. I stammered, "Uh, sure," and went back in the car to reach across to the glove box. I thought, please, please, please, Bark, have your registration in here. And it was. It was all folded up in a small plastic envelope. "Here." I turned around and handed it to him. "Now I have to reach in the backseat to get my license."

He put his hand on his gun and said, "Wait, ma'am. Why do you have newspaper on the back window?" And he opened the back door with the other hand, and there was Hooter tied up with her pants pushed down around the bottom of her butt. *and a smile on her face.*

And before I could even break down and tell him everything about our relationship, I said, "Uh, uh. . ." And shrugged my shoulders. It seemed to say something to him I didn't understand.

I thought I'd just said something akin to, yep, you got me, copper. *Now I've gone beyond ignoring restraining orders, now I'm kidnapping and drugging my ex-girlfriends so I can tattoo embarrassing things on their butts. Take me away.*

But instead, I think he heard something more like, *yep, you got us, copper. We're just a couple of cannibalistic lezzbians from San Francisco, into trendy tied-up sex at the century's end,* because he raised his eyebrows and said, "Uh, you ladies are from San Francisco, I gather?"

I nodded.

He took my identification back to the car with him and I think he must've spent all that time in there writing to his mom, because he came back out and handed my things back to me with a short official filled-out warning form.

"Well, you ladies better move along now."

He looked down at her and she didn't move.

He looked up at me and I did. I tried to run my fingers through my hair, but I was actually ripping them through my hair because it was so tangled. I was so preoccupied with operatic revenge, it might've been weeks since I'd last combed it. Nonchalantly, I said, "Oh, yeah, sorry. She's just passed out. You know how it is the first few months of love. Just sex, sex, sex, until you can't even move!"

And he reached over to put his fingers on her neck and felt her pulse.

"She's just tired," I said.

"Well, yeah. My wife and I were in love once. I understand, I guess. I know you gay people are trying to get your right to get married and all. I s'pose I understand since my dad was in the Black Panthers back in Oakland." He exhaled and took his other hand off his holster and smiled uncomfortably. "Well, you ladies have a nice day," and he walked over to the motorcycle I never even heard pull up.

I waved good-bye, sat back in the car, and rolled another cigarette. But my hands were shaking so badly, most of the tobacco fell out and it was mostly a paper smoke.

Did this mean I should just call it a day, turn back, and go home before it was all too, too late?

I thought about her lies.

I couldn't stop.

I thought about my fifty thousand bucks.

I wouldn't stop.

I thought about the time she called up her dad in Texas to say happy birthday, and he was drunk and told her she was stupid.

I could stop.

I thought about how she used to wait for me to get dressed while she patiently leaned against her car and smoked a cigarette . . . And then another one.

I would stop.

And then I thought about how I always loved that she could shift into third gear with one hand and hold my hand with the other, and then I thought she probably did the same thing with Tule.

I might not stop.

And then I decided to at least do a little something. Just a little token since we were here . . . And I'd come all this way, and all.

After all I did to get here, I tried to reconsider and go through with my plans. But I just couldn't find it in my heart to jerk off over dead bodies. She suddenly just looked so helpless, human, and real, so I just couldn't bring myself to burn anything into her forever. I knew there was a chance that the little Quaker inside of me would sit in civil disobedience until I paid attention and felt shame for the rest of my life if I forever harmed her.

But I was already here. I had to go through with a little token something, take and give a souvenir because I wanted her to remember. Remember something, anything, and know I'm the one who eventually got the last words.

So I took the pen and scribbled TOMATO WAS HERE in big letters across her behind, and tugged her pants back up.

The ocean was beautiful, but I felt my blood wanting to pool in my ankles and make them thick. This isn't what victory felt like, but I figured it might kick in tomorrow morning.

Hooter didn't weigh much even though she was six feet tall and lanky, so I unfolded her down among the craggy bushes along the coast. I knew she'd catch a ride back because Route 1 was a straight shot back home. I checked her wallet and she had about sixty bucks, which I left in there just in case she needed it.

So I folded the padded moving blanket around her gently with the last of my love, and I went back to the car, ripped the gay newspapers off the back windows. I was done. I had nothing else to do but go back to my life and figure out what to do next. That was it. So I pulled away.

So that I wouldn't get stopped by another policeman, I drove very carefully. As if I were driving a stolen car with drugs stuffed in the seats and a dead body in the back.

For the first time in what seemed like weeks, I glanced at myself in the rearview mirror and flinched . . . I usually wore my hair curly, now it had one single dreadlock slab that kept going thwack against the roof of the car with all the wind blowing. I shut the window and it went "thud" on my right shoulder.

And my mouth. I had dried up flaky white drool from I don't know how many nights. Don't know how long it'd been there. If ever I was sexy, I sure wasn't very sexy now. Except maybe to a special dog named Billy from my past. Billy would find me irresistible and lick my face for salt.

I pulled back my lips, and moss. Lots and lots of moss. And I don't know how long they'd been that way.

I'd been a woman lost in a dark, chair-crashing dream of madness, anger, self-righteous moralization, and intellectual bunny slopes. I felt dirty. Like jerking off about something you think is so disgusting afterwards. Dirty and wrong.

I would change everything back to the way it was and pretend nothing happened.

I turned around on the Route 1 perineum, back toward Los Angeles to make things right and bring her back home. But when I got there she was gone. Everything was gone. The only evidence I was ever there was the matching set of tire tracks next to me in the sand and a written warning.

Maybe I never did a thing? Maybe it was all a dream. Yeah. It had to be. The kind of nightmare where you get a written warning, and a second chance in real life.

Thankful, I drove back to San Francisco in my own tule fog.

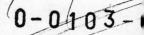

0-0103-

It was only half a day later, early afternoon, and I was sitting at a table in the Mild Side West bar and grill. I was waiting to see if Hooter would show up so I could apologize for everything mean so well that we could pretend nothing bad ever happened.

I'd been at the Mild Side West before with Hooter, in the dawn of our relationship, but I hadn't been there in months and months. The floors were big old wood planks like in my place, and there was a big pool table as you first walked in. White Christmas lights were stapled all over the ceiling, and the best thing about the place was the barber chair that sat next to the video-game machine.

I wanted so hard to feel peace and love for the place and for all humankind, so that when Hooter eventually came in, I'd be wonderful, open, accepting. Nonjudgmental. You get the picture. I'm talking about a picture of love.

But with each beer I ordered, I realized how much I still hated the place because there wasn't a damn thing cute about it. If you really pay attention, it can be a scary, scary place. It's like the House of Wax with Vincent Price as the bartender with long, pendulous gladiator mace breasts that could crush anyone's head against the wall. Only it's not Vincent Price, it's a mean-looking woman and she smokes cigarettes out of the side of her neck.

This bartender was the sort of woman who scares the neighborhood children on Halloween. Not a running away kind of scary, but the kind of deep, shuddering fear that follows you out of your childhood, sits next to you into your adulthood and blows in your ear when you get old. It only finally lets go of you when you're on the edge of your grave and you're wetting yourself. By then you don't even care anyway.

If someone opens the door as you walk by the Mild Side, you will be punched in the stomach with the stench of old cigarettes, rotting alcoholic sweat, and the laughter of scary clown people. It's the kind of loud, phlegmy laugh that can swallow small children's heads. The screams you hear are not those of the little children. No no no. They are the screams of little livers crying for help. But just you walk on by, pardner, because there ain't a thing you can do.

Sitting at home eating handfuls of CoQ10 supplements and giving yourself coffee enemas is not a brilliant alternative. But I think with so much free time, surgically removing outdated organs is a brilliant alternative. You've got your gall bladder, your appendix, maybe some tonsils, and if you live in a bad neighborhood, you might as well get both of your breasts removed. Environmental racism sucks even more when you don't have health insurance.

I want to stand around in a circle with some customers from 7-Eleven and pray. I want to hold their hands and bow our heads in trust that no one's going to grab a handful of the Slim Jims and piss off the cashier.

We will pray for national health care./We will pray for the ability to rejoice in the existence of lesbian bars and liquor stores in the ghettos all over the country./And we will pray for the toxic breasts of women everywhere.

When I finally stopped looking around the place I despised, I was crying in my beer, alone in my little western corner. Crying over the woman I lost and the woman I'd become.

By the time happy hour came around, I'd already been there four or five hours. The bar was pretty full and I could barely make it to the bathroom without swerving. But on my way back to the table, I could've sworn I saw Tule's face from the crowd. But if it was her, she turned around, disappeared out the front door.

Maybe, maybe I was hallucinating, so I got up and swaggered my drunken way toward the front door. A strange thing happened as I started across the room . . . the place seemed to get quieter and a path opened for me to the door. It could have been wishful grande dame thinking, but I swear . . .

When I got outside the dark night air hit me like ice water and pinched my mind awake. I looked around for Tule. I'd parked Bark's Lexus 4x4 right in front of the bar, and the lights were on and the doors were wide open. Someone was in the back. Someone with a flashlight.

Oh my God, I thought, *I never checked with Bark about keeping the car all day.* I figured it was Bark climbing around the back. Maybe cleaning up the mess I left behind.

But as I walked up to the car, I realized it wasn't Bark. Someone much shorter and stockier.

I looked around for help, and I saw a policewoman standing to the side, scanning the street with her eyes. She looked like a no-nonsense kind of *mujer* who drove utility vehicles and had big dogs that behaved. The kind of lesbian who could help you change your flat tire. The kind of lesbian who wanted to do the houseplant thing, but they kept on dying.

Maybe if she just watered them once in a while with her menstrual blood . . . But her girlfriend would more likely be the menstrual-blood kind of lesbian.

"Excuse me," I walked up to her and whispered, "there's someone in my car." I pointed. "There shouldn't be anyone in my car."

"*Your* car?" She said *your* in italics.

"Well, it's not exactly mine, it's my friend's. But I've been driving it—Hey, what's going on?" However, she didn't answer because she was the kind of cop who doesn't answer your questions when she pulls you over.

You answered hers.

Her head flinched back but her neck stayed right where it was. "Come this way, please." And she forcefully pulled me by the arm to the man in the car.

The man looked up when we walked over, "Hey, how ya doin', Tomato?" It was Graciani Valderrama, the policeman who owned the house next to my place. Last I saw of him, he, uh, accidentally built his fence five feet into my yard, until I screamed so much he ripped the posts back out.

"Yeah, I'm fine, I guess." I looked at the lady copper and she let go of my arm.

Graciani laughed and told the lady fuzz, "Well, I found the other glove!"

The lady copper chuckled back and stomped her foot like it was funnier than it was.

"Huh?" I scrunched up my face and asked.

Miss lesbian copper gasped for air like she wasn't too used to this new "laughing thing," and said, "Yeah! Let's see if it fits her!"

They laughed and laughed and when they calmed down, there I was leaning against the car waiting for Godot. "Oh," Graciani waved me away, "it's just a funny cop thing. You wouldn't understand."

"Okay, then, whatever," and I cleared my throat, "Graciani, its nice to see you, but uh. . . What're you doing in my car?"

"Your car? It's registered to a"—and he picked up a short stack of papers—"a mister Bark Flammers out of Texas."

"Well, okay, not my car. But I was driving it."

"Oh yeah?" Graciani slowly got out of the car without taking his eyes off me. He tilted his head and something changed. "You were, eh? . . . For how long, hon."

"All afternoon."

"All afternoon?"

"Yeah, all afternoon."

"Hmm," and Graciani looked at some more papers.

"Oh dear," Graciani said as he took off his police hat. "Is your name really Joline? Does it read," and he leafed through more papers, "Does your driver's license read 'Joline Rodriguez'?"

"Yeah, sure, why?"

"Just a minute," and he turned around and walked a few steps to the police car and got on the police radio. He came back out and shrugged apologetically, "I'm uh, awfully sorry, hon, but we're gonna have to take you in."

"What? In as in you're gonna have to take me *downtown?*"

"Well, we don't really call it downtown anymore . . . "

The woman cop pulled the handcuffs off her belt and unsnapped them.

"Wait, what's this all about?" I jumped back from her.

"Please, Tomato." Graciani walked up and put his hand on my shoulder. "Please, don't make this any harder than it has to be. I'm sure it's all just a mistake and it'll all get cleared up." And he pulled me toward the lady cop. "This is just a formality." He put his hat back on and said, "She has to make sure you don't have any weapons. Hon, it's just a formality."

"What? What? Does Bark think I stole the car? I left him a goddamn note, I didn't steal the car—"

"—hon, hon, it'll all get straightened out once we get to the precinct."

And Graciani went to the Lexus and shut the car doors and said something into his walkie-talkie thing.

"Please raise your arms so we can check you for weapons," the lady cop said firmly.

With Graciani at the car, I turned to run across the street, but I lost my balance and she grabbed me by my shirt and I was down on the hardtop before you could say "How in the hell did Paul Lynde *really* die, anyway?"

I felt her cop foot on my back, pushing me facedown on the ground. A cop foot really does feel different because it also has a little shoe voice that says to you, "I don't think yer gonna be thinkin' of gettin' back up any time soon, ya hear, now?"

The female officer clicked the handcuffs on my wrists behind my back.

I tried to wriggle my wrists out, but they were tight. I burst into tears and wet myself at the same time. "What do you think I am? I watch *Matlock*! I go to bed at nine every night—"

I tried to hide my face as she and Graciani pulled me to my feet. Graciani never said another word to me. Just adopted the stern, sad face of a high school principal who thought you had so much potential, so much on the ball, until he caught you smoking in the parking lot at lunchtime.

I wiped my nose on my shoulder as the lady cop read me my Carmen
Miranda rights and pushed me into the back of the police car. Never
before had I felt so Puerto Rican as I sat there in the back of the
police car, looking out at all the suddenly white faces looking at me.
Even the black one looked white. I didn't think this amount of shame
could possibly, possibly exist and I wanted to take it back. I wanted
no one to see me ever again, and then I had that phlegmy Jerry
Springer guest feeling.

And right there in front of the crowd was Tule. Tule, smoking a
cigarette and holding a glass of beer, watching everything.

Mercifully we pulled away and my hundred-car pileup began.

HAVE SEX WITH SOMETHING:
HUNT IT DOWN AND SIT ON IT.

This./This is what Teddy Pendergrass said when he drove too fast around that curve on Lincoln Drive; this is what Mike Tyson thought as he swallowed that earlobe; this is what Boy George said to himself when he finally told his straight drummer boy that he wasn't really a female and they were having a gay relationship, and this is what I said when they said, Miss Rodriguez, we're booking you for the murder of a woman called Hooter *Mujer*:

Uh oh, I've gone too far.

Stunned, I looked up at the cops and waited for them to say, psych! Only kidding! But cops don't really think anything's funny unless it's Serpico slipping on a banana peel into an oncoming subway car.

"But I thought it was all a dream, and I left her alive!" I told them over and over again. "I swear to God . . . "

And in deep voices they kept saying, *so you're saying you did kidnap her and drive her down on Route 1—*

"Well, yeah, isn't the word *kidnap* a little harsh? We're girlfriends. Or rather, we *were* girlfriends."

They wrote things down and finally just left me alone in the cement room. Graciani wasn't around anymore. I guess he'd begged off on this one.

My pants were wet and stinging, something I hadn't felt since I was a little girl. I didn't want to sit because I wanted to dry out, so I stood with my legs apart and pulled my jeans from my thighs.

Knowing I couldn't charm my way out of this situation in the little cement room was terrifying because this was a game I didn't know how to play. I was glad my mind was still slightly rocking back and forth like a porch swing, from the beers. Now I understood why Hooter drank so much. If feeling like life was also a game she didn't know how to play, I understood. I finally understood, like a knock-knock joke you finally get in the middle of the night.

Hours later they pulled me out of the room and I was finally processed. Fingerprinted and photographed. I was so thankful to be around people again so I could get away from my own head. Maybe that's why they leave you in there so long, so you're desperate to talk.

The man sat me down in a metal chair next to his desk and we could both hear my knees creak. My pants were a cold shock and I confessed everything about loving her, but is that so wrong? And how I got crabs, and how I just wanted to throw eggs at her house and ruin her car engine . . . Before he even rolled the form into the typewriter.

He said a few official-sounding things like I could make a phone call and stuff, but I said, no, no, no phone call, and I told him how

I'd given her my money and that she cheated on me and all I wanted to do was tattoo that I was there on her butt because I didn't want to be forgotten so quickly. I wanted to be famous, because at some point, everyone in San Francisco would have seen Hooter's ass. My name there, forever, but in the end I'd only written on her in pen.

He just listened. Looked like he cared so I told him more. I said I just wanted to leave her there somewhere on Route 1 so she'd have to think of me the whole time she hitchhiked back home with my name on her bottom.

And that when I went back she was gone.

That's when he sat forward and narrowed his eyes on me and said that no, that wasn't it.

He said someone came forward.

Someone came forward? Who could've come forward about writing in pen on her ass? I asked.

And he said, "We're not allowed to tell you."

"You're not?"

"No. But someone saw you."

"Saw me *what?*"

G-0117

"I don't know, you tell me."

"Who saw something?"

"You'll find out before your murder trial, don't worry."

"*What murder?* I didn't kill her."

"Yes you did. We're the police," he said. "We know everything. You can make this easy like Sunday morning, or you can make it hard like a Monday morning." He picked up a Velveeta-colored no. 2 pencil and tapped it on the front of his teeth.

"Sunday morning," I said of course.

"Then where did you dump the body?"

"Body?"

"Yes . . . *body,*" he sighed.

"I told you I left her alive on the side of Route 1—"

"—I told you, you can make this like a Sunday or you can make it like a goddamned Monday morning. The kind of morning where the phone won't stop ringing and you're boss is breathing down your fucking pretty little neck."

My jaw started to tremble and I tried to hold it still. "I already said Sunday, but I didn't dump any body anywhere."

He looked back at his typewriter and started hitting the keys.

I stepped lightly. "So, uh, you know, where did you find her?"

"I can't tell you that," he clipped back at me. He talked like little nail clippers.

"Why not?"

"We're the police, sweetheart. We don't have to tell you much of anything except your Miranda rights." He stood up and ripped the paper out of the typewriter.

"You don't, do you? What about that Freedom of Information Act? Is it only for like a few little things?"

He picked up the pencil can and slammed it back down. It had faded and dusty yarn daisies on it. Brown and Velveeta yellow. There was a theme of cheese, here. Probably made by his little kid back when it was still a little kid. "I'm so sick of you people always talking about your goddamned rights, so shut your damn pie hole and call your lawyer if you're so concerned about *your* murderin' rights."

I thought in a few hours Hooter would show up, and I could go home, so I didn't want to embarrass myself by telling anyone I was here and getting a lawyer.

The policeman leaned forward and whispered that I pushed her over the cliff and into the water. *Now didn't you? Didn't you?* He said over and over again.

"My name is Tomato Rodriguez and I live at 462 Twenty-fourth street—" and I didn't want to say any more about it to him because now this was way more than just a game I didn't know how to play.

The man just looked at me. He had a helmet toupe on and I tried to concentrate on looking for his hairline. Then he turned to his typewriter and started filling out the form, and when he was done, I said, "Can I still make that phone call?"

And then I called my apartment hoping Bark would answer, but he let the machine pick up and I screamed "Pick up! pick up!" but I always leave it turned down so I'm sure he was probably upstairs watching another porn movie.

I left a message asking him to feed my cat. I told him the police had his car and that I was in jail for murdering Hodie. I reassured him that it was an accident and hung up.

The police guy snickered and said to me, *How can pushing a body over a cliff and into the ocean be an accident?*

-0120-0

"But I didn't," I said. "Really, I didn't. I could never roll a body over any cliff." And I was right, because the neighbor on the other side of me was named Bill. Everything about him was pale. Even his attitude. He had blond hair that matched his fleshy pink skin, and he wore a brown motorcycle jacket. Maybe it started out black, but now that he was wearing it, it was brown. Whenever he walked his dogs, he hunched over and looked at the sidewalk through his John Denver glasses. Bill was a creepy loose cannon because he didn't say much, and when he did, he'd lisp and say shout things like, "Things are gonna change around here."

I had many opportunities to kill the Chihuahuas he left at home all day to bark at the slightest noise. I fantasized about cutting their heads off with French guillotines or feeding them big chocolate bunnies. Chocolate's poisonous to dogs. And with all the chocolate bunnies that came my way, I never once tossed them at Bill's Chihuahuas. So there. I was right.

And his rolled his eyes and they said, yeah, lady, tell me another one. And he said, "Come with me," and pulled me back toward the room I'd been in before.

"Wait," I asked, "how long do I have to wait here again? What happens now?" And he just looked at me and smiled. Said nothing, led me inside and I turned around and asked, "You don't even have a body, do you?"

He stood there looking at me and his mouth wanted to say yes, but his eyes said, *no. No, we don't have a body.* "Like I said, hon, I don't have to tell you anything."

"Yeah, that's right, you don't. You're the police, and you know everything, but you don't even know where the body is . . . " And I put my hands confidently on my hips, *"Because there isn't one!"*

"Oh, don't worry, Miss Rodriguez, I'm confident it'll wash ashore." He wouldn't stop smiling and it gave me the creeps.

"—wait," I suddenly realized something and pointed at him, "you have to let me go because you don't even have a body. You've got no proof that I even threw a little goddamn water balloon at her, do you?"

And he chuckled like a scary clown and asked me if I knew a Bark Flammers.

Took me by surprise. "Well, of course I do," I said. "We're friends and that was his car."

Still smiling, he asked, "Is he the same Bark you just called to feed your cat?"

I snorted. "Well, yeah, how many fucking 'Barks' do you think there are?"

"You hired him, didn't you?"

"Well, yeah. So what?"

"Honey," he chuckled, "he's a well-known professional."

"Well, don't you think I knew that?" He raised his eyebrows at that. Mistaking it for his being impressed I went on. "I mean, for God's sake, maybe I didn't know he was so *well known*, as you say, but so fucking what?"

He laughed and pointed at me. "Nice to know you're so open. This could really help you out. Would you being willing to let me tape record you saying this all over again?"

I got up off the floor. "Sure, I don't give a shit."

"Now, you're sure you don't want a lawyer, right?"

"What do I need a lawyer for?"

"Okay." He smiled and said he'd be right back.

When he returned, he set up a two tiny microphone stands and pushed the red RECORD button on the tape recorder.

He asked me some general questions about my name and address and then he asked me if I knew Bark Flammers. Yes, I said. Did I hire him? Yes, I said.

He asked if I'd hired Bark Flammers to murder Hooter.

"What?"

"You heard me, and don't give me any malarkey."

"No!" I slapped my palms on the table for emphasis. "I hired him to help me do things like drag her naked over shag carpeting until she got rug burns, and then rub saltwater all over . . . That kind of thing. You know . . . Exact a more ruthless revenge on her."

"What could be more ruthless than killing her?" He gave me a too-smug look.

"Well, that would have been pointless, wouldn't it?" I stared at him. "The point of revenge is them suffering with the consequences as long as possible. Even Doctor Claw's got nothing left to do once he blows up the world. You've gotta keep your adversaries alive or else there's nothing left to do except take up gardening and think about what you've done until you're disgusted with yourself—"

"—well, maybe you should've been more like Doctor Claw. Looks like *you'll* be suffering the consequences."

"Look, I didn't kill her. I'm not a fucking murderer. My name is Tomato Rodriguez and I live at 462 Twenty-fourth street . . . My name is Tomato Rodriguez and I live at 462 Twenty-fourth street . . . "

"Well, we already talked to your Bark Flammers and he already told us that you hired him to do away with Hooter for cheating on you. The way he figured it was you were trying to frame him and he didn't want any part of your mess."

He rocked back on the sturdy wooden chair and put a cigarette in his mouth. "And, lady, you might've gotten away with it too, because he's a bad man, but you made a mistake going through with it after that highway patrolman checked up on you." He leaned forward and lit the cigarette. "Add our eyewitness account of you throwing the body over the cliff and"—he sucked on the cigarette—"it's curtains for you, sweetheart," he said through a stream of smoke. "I couldn't ask for a nicer retirement party present."

"*What eyewitness account?* And . . . And . . . Bark Flammers?" And then I started crying again because now I felt like I was standing helpless in the middle of a haunted house with a blindfold so I could just hear the doors slamming shut, listen to the chandeliers crash to the floor, feel objects whiz by me, and smell the blood pouring from all the water faucets.

He hit STOP as my band played on, and scooped the recorder up with the microphones and left me alone with my rat-trapped mind to play the what-if game.

What if some midwestern crazed tourists stopped by the road immediately after I pulled out, saw Hodie's drugged body and tossed it over the edge for kicks. Right now they were headed back to Nebraska and I was left holding the bag? Or worse, what if I did one of those crazy blackout things you hear about on Columbo where someone doesn't even remember shooting someone and putting the gun in the body's hand? I had to admit that I hadn't exactly been my usual charming self lately.

I had to admit, that one *was* entirely possible.

Suddenly, my crazy thoughts were interrupted as the door swung open and I was escorted by two quiet uniformed men down to a bunch of cells where they mumbled some words to another man and left. The man had me take off my jewelry and empty all my pockets, and he put it all into a manila envelope. Then he asked for my shoelaces and walked me down to a cell with a woman who'd stolen a refrigerator.

She was shaped like a big ice cream cone, wore a faded jean jacket, and had thin, brown, stringy hair that stuck to her scalp. There were two long cot things on either side of the cell that looked like giant burnt cookie sheets, and she sat leaning against the wall on one of them.

I waved hello and sat on the other. She said her name, but I forget it now, and she started telling me that her landlord sent her here for moving a refrigerator from an empty apartment to hers. That it was her family's fault she was there. They'd told on her. Her mom was out to get her. So they sent her to jail. She repeated everything but her name over and over again until finally she fell asleep.

That's when I decided to pee. The open toilet was right there between these two baking pans. It was worse than any gas station bathroom I'd ever, ever seen going cross country and built so cruelly high, a girl had to be six feet tall to squat without touching the edge. I almost wish I'd kept my little crab friends so they could loyally do battle for me against all the germs writhing and multiplying on the porcelain.

I gently placed one boot on the edge of the crusty porcelain bowl and jumped up so I could stand my foot on the other side, pull my pants down and squat.

But without shoelaces to keep it snug, my big boot wobbled so my foot slipped into the toilet water. And like Anne Rice's vampires, I just had to give into that this is where I was now and it couldn't possibly get any filthier.

I peed and wiped myself with sheets of water-stained brown paper towels scattered behind the toilet. Right then I really knew why they took your shoelaces and belts away. Because if I even had a ribbon in my hair, I'd have hung myself with it. But I guess if I were the kind of girl to wear ribbons in her hair, I wouldn't even be here. I'd be out buying more ribbons.

I slipped off my boot and set it against the bars so it could dry up, and I curled up on my baking pan and tried to sleep.

But I didn't sleep because at something like midnight, the night was still young, and the place started filling up. First with men on the other side of the wall talking about the girls they wanted to fuck.

Thankfully, the more women that filled our side, the less I heard the men laughing and shouting on the other. Women came in for selling drugs and even later on, prostitutes were in cells next to ours, talking about their pimps and how they were jealous of his new girl who he let sleep in his room with him. I didn't really want to listen because it was like changing channels when the news comes on.

I fantasized about hanging myself with my hair, but it wasn't nearly long enough (although the hair on my legs was. But I wasn't so limber). Maybe if I tried to jump off the toilet headfirst. High, but not nearly high enough. I didn't because it'd be just my luck that I'd survive as a drooling vegetable, and then Hooter would come forward and just say *what's all the fuss about?* Because she'd gone camping or something, and there I'd be, stuck screaming inside my head, locked in some snake pit for the rest of my life.

Oh, even that would've been preferable to this.

Faced with the idea that maybe I *had* murdered my ex-girlfriend, I decided that I'd better get ready for the big house.

I decided to call myself *Mad Dog.*

My name would be long like a worm. Adding *Mad Dog* to Joline Tomato Gertrude Rodriguez would add another inch, and when you're reaching for that g-spot, sometimes an inch makes *all* the difference. You girls know what I mean. And, if I was innocent, and not a victim of fashionably repressed memory, an inch is an inch is an inch.

That's why women with long fingers make me nip around at their ankles for a little attention. Six foot tall women have the kind of fingers that can make you moo like a cow and swear like a six-year-old. Now they don't show *that* in Hollywood movies, do they? No. It's a secret.

I wanted to proudly be a bottom. Feel no shame, because if you're a bottom, no one knows how bad you are in bed. My mistake was trying to give a little bit back to America.

I didn't think this might be the kind of place you want to have that kind of epiphany, because look at all the bad things that happened to Linda Blair, although I hear that she's working with horses up in Connecticut now.

Then I went back to trying to talk myself into believing I was somehow protecting myself and my honor in doing what I did to Hooter. Goddamned Argentinean honor, and I don't even have any family there.

But the self-righteousness thing doesn't last long when you've killed someone and you're sitting in jail. A little drunk with wet pants.

Still, another drunker part of me felt free, felt bad, evil, and like my threats weren't hollow. When you've committed murder, what law won't you break?

When I was a tiny little kid I looked at my great-great-grandfather and wondered if he'd ever killed a man. I didn't understand how you could get through life without accidentally killing another person, like accidentally breaking a candy dish. And when my mom said you went to jail for killing someone, I thought I'd be sure to accidentally kill someone because people are fragile.

And here I was, waiting for hours in a cement-block room after accidentally killing a fragile person I once adored and committed myself to in a women's clinic where they had three different size plastic specula on the wall for sale. Women loving women and admiring each other's secret cervixes.

Like a common murderer, I'd rolled her body out of the car and covered it with a moving blanket, like in so many bad, bad movies before me, and then thrown it into the ocean.

Or something.

Oh God, it was hell not remembering.

Then some fat lady guard in stretchy blue chinos that were way too tight, started rolling a cart down the aisle, passing out American cheese sandwiches on white bread wrapped in wax paper and Styrofoam cups of Kool-Aid.

Ah, Kool-Aid. Kool-Aid was so perfect for my new life.

I wasn't hungry and I just left my food on the ledge in the bars. Within seconds, roaches were diving into my Kool-Aid and ripping into the wax paper without even asking. But they left my boot alone.

I didn't dare wake up my refrigerator friend because I didn't want her to get a sugar rush from the Kool-Aid and start talking about how her family was out to get her again, so I just let the roaches have her share too.

Most of the other girls laughed like this was really a cool theme-party, threw their food into the gutter on the other side of the aisle and that's when I noticed the metal sign above the gutter that read DO NOT THROW FOOD.

But that's why we were all here, wasn't it? Because we weren't listening to any of the signs.

MEAT DOG

In the morning they crossed our arms and chained us together in groups of four. My quartet walked sideways to a little police van. We were all going to a hearing at some other building and in some kind of big courtroom, we filled up all the rows of benches. I sat next to a black girl with boils on her neck. I'd only heard about boils and I wondered how you got them on your neck, but I didn't want to ask her.

It was like the first day of school when you're the new kid and everyone else already knows each other. People were laughing and shaking hands, asking about each other's friends and family members. If last night was what being locked up was like, why did people come back once they knew how it was?

Was this life after Jerry Springer? If so, Jerry Springer was passing out blankets covered in smallpox and we were asking for matching pillows.

A door opened up on the back wall, and a rotund woman in a tea-length black judge's robe marched out. She wore stockings and a pair of black suede Birkenstocks, which instantly gave away her liberal tendencies. This didn't mean much, as liberals sometimes want to hand stiff sentences to teach irritatingly caring lessons, while conservatives might just want to get the whole day over so they can go get changed and make it to some fund-raising dinner.

Everyone went up before the judge and they were kept in custody or sent somewhere else, but mostly they were let go and given a court date.

By the time I went before the judge for my own arraignment and bail hearing, just about everyone was gone, and it was obvious the police had talked to neighbors about me because some lady in a suit stood up behind a table and read statements from a file. They knew about my accidentally burning the effigies of Hooter and Tule in front of the German lady's house; they had the Chihuahua man as a witness to my kidnapping Hodie; and they had an anonymous witness to my dragging Hodie's body to the edge of the cliff on Route 1 and pushing her over the edge.

Anonymous witness? I screamed out loud by accident, and the judge slammed her gavel down. "But I didn't kill her!" I cried. "I just drugged her and she was—"

An old guard in a brown uniform walked toward me and I shut up with a whimper. I looked around, but no one was going to help me out. Not even the girl with boils on her neck.

Then a man in a suit fine enough to make us all look like we were wearing polyester pants and acrylic sweaters with pills on the arms (which we probably were, now that I think about it), stepped up beside me and announced that he was my attorney. As he opened his expensive leather briefcase, he suggested that because of the passionate nature of the crime, I be committed to some new/improved halfway house since I was a professional artist represented by a gallery, for whom he worked, and had no prior record.

"Uhm, excuse me, but don't forget the bail part," I whispered loudly toward my lawyer. He just kept spewing legal jargon to the judge but I wasn't hearing any numeric bottom line that would set me free.

Then I just blacked out and lost track because I couldn't get over the fact that I was even in this situation. It all just started becoming "Ginger, blah blah blah."

Whatever it was he said about psychiatric observation in the halfway house, the judge agreed. They set a court date for nine months later and away I went. To the place they call The Zucchini Cave.

My well-dressed lawyer winked at me, clicked shut his briefcase, cheerfully said he'd get back to me later, and waved bye, saying "Hang in there, Sunshine! I'll talk to you later."

"But wait!—What about bail? Hey! Who's this witness?" I cried after him.

He blew me a kiss, then he was out the doors.

He was a lawyer—my lawyer—but he was no Matlock. Matlock would've taken me home, made some chicken, and played the guitar. I wondered what my lawyer's name was. And why he was blowing me good-bye kisses. No one from New York blows kisses. It's just not natural.

ANAL BEADS FOR THE TIMID

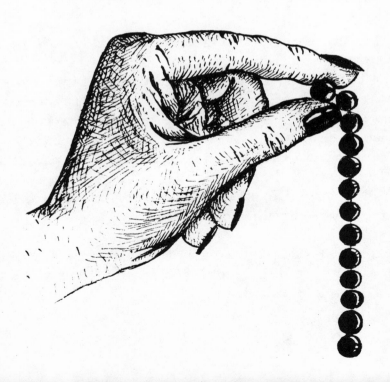

Going to jail's like going to New York. At first you're kind of like *golly-gee-willickers! This is New York.* And then before long you're just like the rest of them, stifling a yawn and thinking *Big deal. Impress me.*

That's what jail's like.

First, you're impressed with how gross it is. Then you think that the welcoming committee gives you cavity searches with broken plastic forks just for fun, just like New York tourists think you get bludgeoned the moment you enter the subway.

Reality's different: girls behind bars aren't really so, so scary. They're way scarier out there in real life because there aren't any guards around to tell them to cut it out. But there's this whole tule fog of myth around these birds in a cage that we're supposed to believe the same way we're supposed to believe Hollywood's really overrun by heterosexuals. Prison's really no worse than trying to get through your first year of junior high in the Bronx, thinking you're finally talking like a real Puerto Rican, when a tough Rican girl named Sugar looks at you funny one day and asks, what're you anyway?—Dominican or something?

Trying to become a black girl worked better for me. Talking in ebonics is way easier than pulling off "the Puerto Rican who's lived in New York all her life" sound.

I first became a black girl at the age of ten. I was going to a grade school in Amherst, Massachusetts, because I was living with my father. Back then I moved more often than I changed the channel. Anyway, it was the nicest-looking grade school I've ever seen.

I remember it was so nice, Bill Cosby even had his kids driven there from Greenfield in a chocolate brown Mercedes.

But other than his kids, most of the black girls in school were kind of like white trash. Their moms were all looking for love in all the wrong places and their sisters in high school were having kids and chasing their lying boyfriends down the streets with multicolored Japanese cars.

And while all the white kids looked like child eunuchs who'd grow up to lose their virginity at safely tragic times like in all the Judy Blume books, the black girls were the first ones to wear bras and sharpen their attitudes like knives.

Since this school was in a progressively thinking college town, our black teacher, Miss Jackson, got a lot of support from the staff to start a club. It was to be the official black support club. The idea was to have a little support group so black kids wouldn't grow up with bad self-esteem problems in a whitey-white world and end up in jail for accidentally murdering some lesbian lover (let's just say for example).

Miss Jackson was definitely black and beautiful and had enough bracelets on her arms that she sometimes got bruises. According to the sixth graders, she had so many clothes that you wouldn't see the same outfit twice in one year.

I wanted to turn out just like Miss Jackson, but after five days it turned out to be too much work wearing anything other than the clothes I'd left on the floor the night before.

And when Miss Jackson pulled me out of class to go to the black support group, I felt it was only right to tell her *but my mom, she's white.* I told her, she's so white, she welts up if you hug her. She shook her head like *this, this is what white society has done to our black children: made them deny who they really are.*

Miss Jackson shook her head furiously, seriously, and her hundreds of bracelets jingled as if to say, *Look at yourself, girl. Look at yourself, sister, don't be ashamed anymore.* Then Miss Jackson pointed to my arm.

I looked at my arm. Indeed, it was kind of a dark beige. No . . . Even darker than that . . . In fact, some might say it was the color of a cardboard box. A blaxploitation producer would've said "brown sugar," but back then I was only ten.

I looked back up at Miss Jackson, then back at my arm. She put her arms around my head and pulled me to her. Like my mom, she was from the generation that wanted to make the world a better place, and she made me feel the same way I did when my mom and her friends wanted to teach me to love my reproductive system. She made me want to grow up black and be proud of my vagina at the same time, which is difficult if you grow tits too soon and spend a lot of time around a lot of black men three times your age.

I wanted to give in and believe, especially with her rocking me back and forth like that. Her bracelets were crushing my ear, but that's the only pain I felt as I turned into a black girl.

However, I didn't even know what soul food was and I couldn't slip in and out of a southern accent like a Sunday dress along with the rest of the girls. I tried to sleep facedown to take the point out of my nose, but I still talked like a white girl who didn't know how to dance.

So, sometimes I wasn't entirely convinced about the black thing. But in the end we all really want to be black anyway, even though none of us wants to be paid or followed around a store like one. I was black and proud. I even got myself a black fist pick and started drawing pictures of African women in big earrings in the margins of my math papers.

Then Miss Jackson took us black people to the section of the books by black people. That's where I first read stories about poor black boys falling out of windows by accident while their older brothers were making toast by holding pieces of bread stuck on a fork over a gas stove, and I thought wow, being black is going to suck big time.

It had to suck for me, too. I couldn't wait to join the ranks of oppression and pain. The kind where you might as well lie back, because it's not your fault.

Looking back, it was the ultimate s/m experience for a little girl who would later try bulimia but find it too much work because you've got to plan after-dinner conversation around your digestion, and I wanted to get lost in the swirling whirlpool of recognized victimization. Why be an unnoticed victim? Why be a martyr if no one notices? And being brought up Quaker, I believed that there are no Academy Award ceremonies in the afterlife.

And thinking that then, I looked for instances of prejudice. It's the subtle oppression that'll get you, my brother. I was so mad at white people. Hate hate hate. Bad bad bad. I was ashamed of my freckled mom for repeatedly buying houses in good school districts. I was ashamed of my freckled white mom for being related. I thought of ways of pretending I wasn't related to her, that she was someone else's mom when she visited me.

I scraped up every excuse I could to disapprove of my mother. When I'd lived with her, why hadn't she sent me to the Camden public schools system, where kids routinely graduate high school without making it through Dick and Jane?

My evil white mom. She'd pulled me away from the solidarity of suffering with my people, and it wasn't long before welfare became sexy and having a big Puerto Rican husband who cheated on me and beat me up was what I wanted. I wanted to suffer more so I could have my own *look-I'm-oppressed* stories and get the Academy Award in the afterlife for "Best Unsupportive Actress."

Even at my ripe old age, I may not believe in awards in the afterlife, but I do believe that someday I'm going to have to pay for putting my mom through hell. And pay *big*.

But I was young, black, and armed with beginner tampons and a love for my vagina, so I studied and planned for my victimized future.

I noticed that instead of happening in homogenized-milk Canada, the bad black stories always happened in New York, and so I thought black people were in New York making toast without toasters, doing heroin, falling out of windows, and being picked up by the police as often as I took the school bus.

So then I wanted to move to New York when I turned eleven. I wanted to go live with my grandmother in the Bronx so I could get in touch with My People. No more detached housing with big backyards for me.

I thought wow, New York. Place in the stories. Will the police ignore my rights and bash in my cardboard-colored head? Would I make toast by hanging bread over a burner? Will one of my family members be driven insane by the poverty and jump out the window, even though we lived on the first floor?

But once I was there, it was just like any place else. People waved hello, cars stopped when you crossed the street, and we had a toaster. So, I forgot I was in New York, and once in a while, I'd think, "Oh, yeah, I'm in New York, it's supposed to be like Stevie Wonder's higher ground."

The only time I remembered I was in the Bronx was when I went a few blocks away to my aunt and uncle's house and they got stoned in front of the kids who were already bouncing off the walls from all the Kool-Aid.

And then I thought, wow. Here I am living in New York. Living just enough, just enough for the city. Yeah. Chocolate city. And that's where the girl named Sugar thought I was really a Dominican. Or something.

All the books make it sound like moms in the Bronx beat their kids to wake them up for school. There were so many moms there who took better care of their kids than moms in the suburbs who might've drunk too much and run to aerobics class as soon as the kids got home. Moms who let their boyfriends fondle their daughters. Shit-faced dads who woke up their sons with shotguns in their faces an hour before the school bus came. Creepy, creepy, shit.

And since no one talks to each other in the suburbs, you only hear about this stuff when their kids get stoned, corner you in the park, and talk way too much, and then you want them to shut up because you already got the creeps from reading those old oppressed black stories.

It's high time some of those kids pull the sheets back on the suburbs because there was some really *wrong* shit going on. The kind of shit that would've made Gidget run *to* the Bronx, so she could live just enough, just enough for the citaaay.

Anyway, it turns out that Miss Jackson married a blond-haired, blue-eyed man named Bill, and I felt betrayed. She betrayed the cause.

And that even happens now if you're a lesbian and sleeping with a man. You've gone to the other side. And if you've tried to cover your sexual bases by claiming up front that you're bisexual, you're only bisexual until you sleep with a man. Everyone wants you to choose for the cause, just like a ten-year-old girl the color of a cardboard box.

VEGETARIAN

PORN

Suffice it to say, Zucchini Cave was a nice place compared to the city jail. It was a lot like that grade school with the carpeting, except it was green. Everything was green, we even wore green when we first got in there. That's why we were referred to as zucchini girls.

And since it was a correctional experiment, there weren't a lot of zucchini girls around yet, maybe only sixty or seventy, so it was like going to the Jersey shore in the fall. You kind of had the place to yourself and it seemed like everywhere we went, there was just a handful of us.

The main part of the building was a monstrous and new liberal reform project prepared to accommodate something like a thousand bad girls. You could tell. You could've been dropped repeatedly on your head as a baby and still notice all the good intentions: bouquets of silk flowers spread around the building in stainless steel vases firmly bracketed to the wall, color-coordinated stripes on the floor to point you in the right direction, because just like in the hospital, we were all there to get better.

In the foyer, you could see the rare, framed photos of a giggling Lolita Lebron, or Squeaky Fromme shaking some mayoral candidate's hand. Imitation brass plaques were cemented underneath each photo, with a brief description and a comment about how rehabilitation can be fun. But something didn't seem quite right about seeing these first two photos, followed with a shot of Dr. Jean Tarnower playing what appeared to be a lively game of charades with Leona Helmsley. I couldn't put my finger on it . . . but as I passed through and looked a little closer, it seemed that shadows were falling on a couple of women in very different directions in the same photo. Huge, toothy smiles on faces where the eyes just didn't scrunch up. And that ain't natural. There was just something that rang a little "Adobe Photo Shop" about the whole thing. Call me cynical, call me paranoid, but I find it difficult to believe in the veracity of some picture of little Amy Fisher smiling and waving while baking an industrial-size batch of cookies in a prison kitchen.

And the former detention center for girls was now an additional wing that had formerly been a high school built in the late sixties. All sorts of green metal panels underneath the crank windows. Greens in every shade. That's how this place got the nickname Zucchini Cave.

They let me finally scrape off my now disgusting clothes and take a shower. They hosed me off for lice and poked and squirmed their fingers around in every possible orifice, looking for hidden closet space.

A big, elderly woman in a hair net walked over to me with a bundle and an empty net bag. "You can wear regular clothes here, so you might want to have yours brought over from home. But for now you can wear these, and we'll put your old clothes in the wash." I put my clothes in the net bag and she pinned a metal tag with a stamped number at the top. "Here," she handed me a cardboard square and told me it was like a claim check. Then she gave me a pile of green clothes that looked like scrubs from a hospital, and I was led down the hall to my tank. A small room with two sets of bunk beds and a small window.

All basic prison-movie first-day stuff.

There were two small jitterbugs in the cell, sitting quietly on the bunk on the other side of the room. They wore wide-striped clothes from 1983 with puffy shoulders and terry cloth trim. The girls were small and when you looked at them, you thought, this is why some people think all dogs basically look alike. What do I mean? It's a species thing; you wouldn't understand. Anyway, one girl had cut her hair short and dyed it blond. Looked like a baby chick. The other girl looked like—now follow me, here—sort of like a white girl trying to be a black girl looking like a white girl.

She wore gold toaster earrings and straightened her hair and re-curled it into a monstrous thick single curl over her forehead and pulled it into four ponytails on top of her head, and lined her naked mouth in brown eyeliner so her lips would look bigger and you'd know her mouth was there. Like a chocolate milk mustache.

All in all, they were like the nondescript extras in the background of a TV show about a girl named Jeb who could barely keep her family fed.

But who was I to talk? It was the late nineties and here I was just finally starting to like Debby Harry and Grace Jones for the first time.

They just nodded and said hello and went back to reading.

When I put my stuff down on the bunk a tall black girl came in. She looked like the kind of girl who liked her groceries.

"Who are you?" she demanded.

Forcing myself to slowly look her up and down, I noticed she wore a pair of green cotton drawstring pants covered in ballpoint pen scrawl, and on top she wore a wife-beater T-shirt. The ribbed kind. And on the top of her left arm was tattooed a heart and a banner through the middle that said *Big Daddy Bob*. I clicked my teeth and tried to keep the half-lidded thing going. "My name's crazy," I started, and popped a generic cigarette in my mouth. "Crazy, wild, *insane Mad Dog*." I lit it and squinted at her through the smoke as I exhaled. "What's yours?"

She waved the smoke out of her face. "Oh a wiseguy, eh? Yeah, well, they call me Bobby Zadora." And she walked over to my stuff, threw it on the floor, and pulled my mattress off and dropped it on the bottom bunk. "But you can just call me Bob . . . " And she lay down on both mattresses. "*Big Daddy Bob*."

"Why do they call you big? Huh, Bob? Because your ideas are big? Because your head is big? Because your ass is big . . . ?" Sometimes it's all about posturing and all you've gotta do is not look scared. Like going up to a gang and asking for a light because you're not scared, even though you're getting rings of sweat under your arms.

"You'd better wise up sister." Big Bob yawned. "I got a funny feeling this is how you landed yourself here in the clink."

So I wiped a long curl from my face and sighed. I didn't intend to say anything back, but like I said, being bad and going to prison makes you speak in tongue. Tongue stolen from a bad drive-in movie: "Yeah, well none of it's your business, is it? Maybe you could've welcomed me with a plate of cookies or a nice hug, but *no*. So, I'm gonna do you a favor and knock your pretty little teeth so far down your throat, you're gonna get a picket fence around your asshole."

"Don't walk away from me, you chalk-faced ho'!"

Now, let me just say for the record that she was wrong on a couple of counts there. First, I wasn't walking away. In fact, I was too scared to even turn my back on her. Second, I'm not, nor have I ever been, chalk-faced. In wintertime I may get a bit pale sometimes, but being half Puerto Rican, I can only get so pale.

I think that might've just been her warrior cry because before I was about to argue, she bull-headed me in the stomach and knocked the wind out, leaving me unable to ask what town she was from or what her favorite color was.

When I caught my breath from the floor I found myself uncontrollably saying, "You're like the boys in grade school who used to punch you to say they liked you."

Then she came over and kicked me while I was down. She threatened to make me her toilet pig girl, and since I didn't want to know what that was, I finally shut my pie hole.

I went out into the common area which they liked to fake us out by calling it the living room. There was a whole fiberboard bookshelf with make-believe wood grain, filled with books for us to read. They mostly looked like Oprah book-club selections.

And because most crimes by women are committed out of passion against someone they know, the bookshelf also held a lot of books on enjoying nonmonogamy so you wouldn't get quite so pissed and blow his head off when your man cheats on you.

So I sat down to read the books on nonmonogamy in the hopes I would come to embrace the idea of polyfidelity, and become more peaceful even though the horse had long since left the barn with my fifty grand.

I hadn't been reading long before I realized that flighty people were writing these books on how to be nonmonogamous, polyfidelitous, polyamorous. And everyone gives bisexuals a bad, confused rap. It didn't take a rocket scientist to figure they were blowing most of their brain power on creative *terms* for nonmonogamy.

Polyamorous people feel sorry for those "poor monofidelitous people who just are so small-minded and don't know how to get beyond themselves." I tried to feel myself becoming one of those poly-love people shaking a tambourine and waiting for the love sheets to get out of the dryer.

But it was a big fat lie. Once you make a down payment on a place in Argentina, you can't go back home and spin around like fringe in a Stevie Nicks video.

With nothing else to do, I kept to myself, and figured out how to get back at Big Bob Zadora. Some TV show came on about an adventure guy who'd gotten caught in an avalanche. He smoked Lucky Strikes for ten days in the small pocket of air and disinfected his wounds with his own urine. There we go. Just like the eighties. He wrote a book about it. Became a best seller. Just like the nineties.

And that's when I got another brilliant idea. The kind of idea that jammed-up like a hundred-car pileup and got me here in the first place.

So that night I slept on the top bunk without my mattress. Now, this wouldn't have worked if it was a baking pan bed. No, I would've just soaked in it myself. No, the bottom was all springs. In the middle of the night when everyone was asleep, I wiggled out of my pants, sat up and peed. Peed, peed, peed. Not a big pee, but a little, ambitious pee. The last of my own expensive vitamins all over Big Bob Zadora.

I lay back down and started snoring. But Big Bob didn't buy it and she jumped up, sat on me and started twisting my tit. "Whistle or lose it!" she demanded.

I screamed for her to stop in the name of humanity, and she said, oh you're really breakin' my heart. Finally a guard came over and pounded on the door for us to settle down.

Big Bob jumped back down to her bunk and I said, "There. Down, Big Butt Zadora."

"I'm gonna get you, bitch, and the name's Big Bob."

"Keep your goddamn mitts off me. What're you gonna do, Big Butt? Make me have anal sex with you in the showers or something? Make me, uh, toss your salad?"

"Oooh, that's if you're *lucky*, my little toilet pig." And so she said, "One thing I'm gonna learn you, is that if you want to run with the big dogs you can't piss like a puppy."

"Look," I said, "you may be able to scare Linda Blair or Leona Helmsley with that shit, but not me." There I was speaking in tongues again. I had no control over what came out anymore.

"What?"

I wanted to say *I'm so sorry, I don't know what came over me. Can we just forget everything and get to sleep?* But instead I found myself saying, "Oh, don't *what* me, young lady, or I'll give you something to *what* me about!" Why couldn't I shut the hell up? I was channeling the spirit of a battered wife queen from ancient Egypt.

"Bitch, you'd better zip it up!"

I jammed my face in the pillow and mumbled into it, and thankfully she didn't hear. So she just got up and turned all the bedding over and went back to sleep.

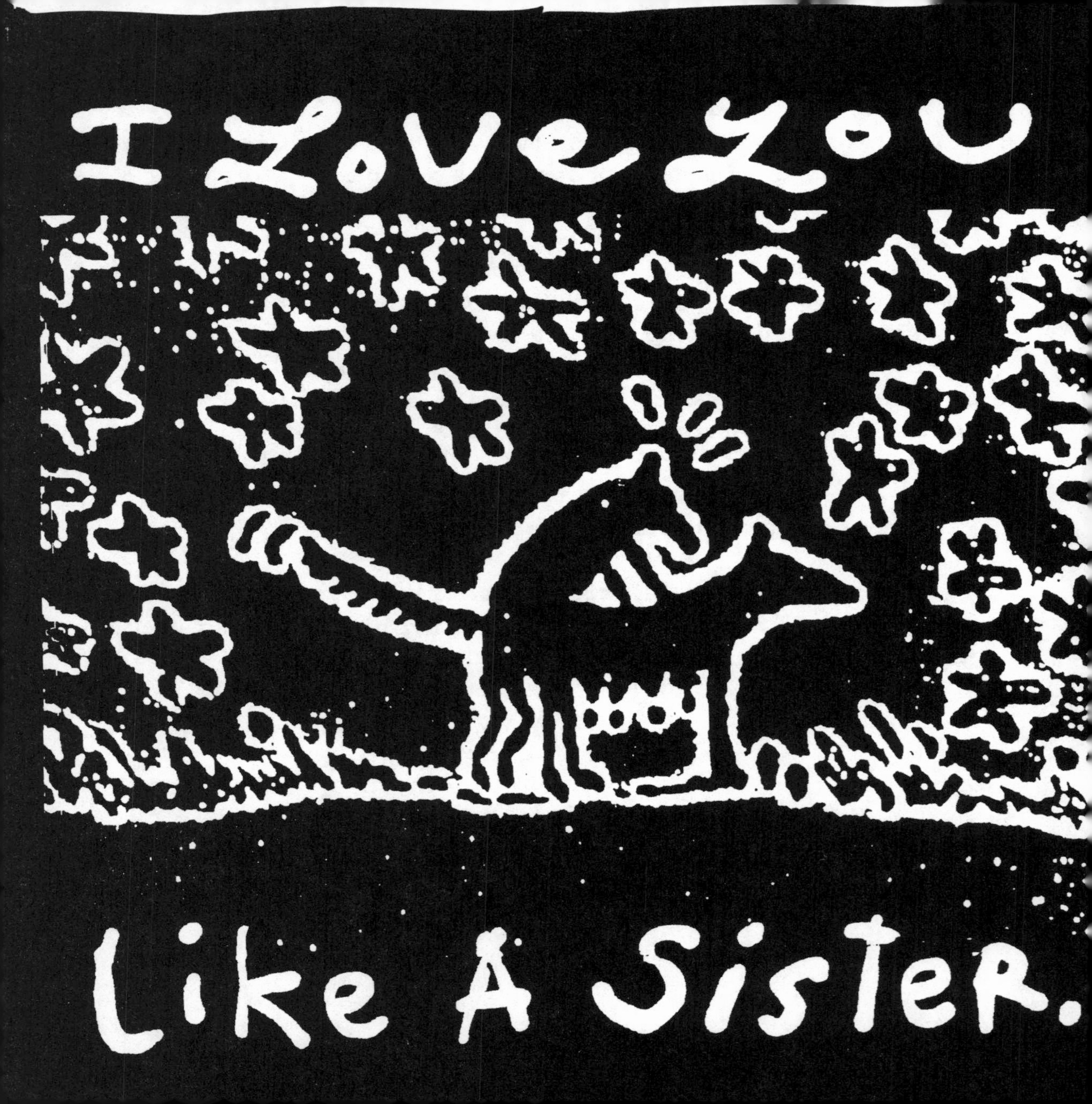
I Love You
Like A Sister.

One of the things you'll learn from an Oprah show, is to go to an authority figure if someone's bullying you. Now I think you'll be in worse trouble if you tell, unless they're the kind of bullies that end up on the news for throwing a kid out of a window or setting him on fire, so just become friends with an authority figure. Yeah, buy the authority figure a drink, and you're better off.

So after having black-and-blue arms for two weeks, that's what I did with a nun who worked there as a kind of counselor. What she wanted to be was the big sister of America. The biggest.

She said her name was May, to call her Sister May, but don't say any "Sister May I" jokes because she's already heard them all. Sister May was one of those down-to-earth/I've-seen-it-all nuns who wasn't mean like a woman in charge.

She took care of me. Sister May was everything I ever wanted in a sugar daddy, a sugar mama. All except for the money thing. You never get the money for free anyway. You've got to do housework and spit out kids, or give the kind of blow jobs that give you a flabby throat. Nothing's free. Even you twenty-seven-year-olds still living at home know exactly what I mean.

0-01#7-0

No, she was kind of quiet, a little stocky, and had a strong face, like she'd automatically know what to do with a full bladder and a pack of smokes in case of an avalanche. And being a Quaker, I didn't know you weren't supposed to tell nuns raunchy jokes in public, but she didn't mind. In fact she pressed her lips to keep from smiling and looked down most of the time, as if to tell God she wasn't really paying attention.

And I thought, this wasn't really jail. There's carpeting.

DEVIL GIRL

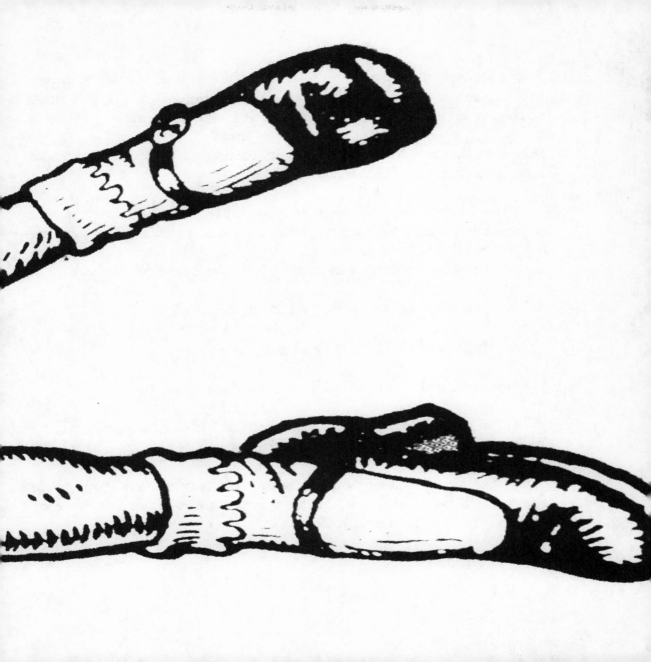

Visiting day was once a week on Saturdays, and I didn't expect anyone, but a guard came in and politely tapped on the cell door while I was reading, and said someone was here to see me.

Maybe it was my New York lawyer, coming to blow me a kiss and finally pick me up from school.

I skipped down the hall next to the guard who led me to a nice carpeted room covered in glass bricks on the outside wall. Lots of bright sunlight shone in on the Plexiglas, and there was a glare across it and everything was so new. Not even scratched up yet.

Bark Flammers was sitting on the other side.

"You stinkin', filthy rat! Why, I oughta—"

"—hey, chill out, Rodriguez."

"Yeah, well, if I was you, I'd beat feet and quick. And don't call me Rodriguez. They know me as Mad Dog here."

"Hey, Sad Dog, what're you stuck in a bad movie? Are you going for a fat heroin chic look, or have you got yourself a couple of shiners? What's it all about, Bad Dog?"

"Why I oughta—"

"Oh, what're you gonna do to me from over there? Press your ass against the plastic so you look like grocery meat? Let me tell you right now, that won't be pretty. Well, listen: I was kinda hopin' you weren't sore." He held up a stuffed duffel bag. "I brought your clothes."

"Yeah, well fuck you and the horse you rode in on."

"Hey, can I talk to you? I can't talk to you as long as you talk like a bad movie. So can I talk to you?"

I folded my arms and crossed my legs. "Sure, help yourself."

"Well I'm thinkin' you're out trying to pull a fast one on me, using my car, leaving evidence all over it. When I do one of my stunts, there are no slipups. That's why I'm out here and you're in there. It would've been curtains for me, takin' the fall for you just because you didn't wanna pay me."

"What? There was no fall. I didn't kill her."

"Isn't that what you hired me to do?"

"What? Kill her? You've got to be kidding."

"Yeah. That's what you said: *Do the big bang. Do the deal, go all the way.*"

"What in the hell are you talking about, Flammers?"

"Well, what exactly do you think I do for a living? Sneak into fancy gyms, find aging baby boomers on treadmills and eat fried chicken and ice cream in front of them? No way! I'm a professional and no matter what you've read, I don't do things like that anymore—not ever since that accident, anyway—look, the way I see it is you called me up in Texas to do away with your girlfriend. You didn't want to just slash her tires anymore, you wanted to, and I quote you, 'do the big bang.' I've got it on tape and that's what I gave to the police to keep my ass out of the sling."

"What?"

"Oh yes, darling, I tape all my phone conversations at the office."

"Wait, what is this 'big bang'?"

"Oh, don't play stupid with me, missy."

"No, really. I don't know."

"You don't have to pretend. I'm not tape recording this."

"I don't care. I still don't know what it is."

He shrugged. "It's what you said you wanted."

"No I didn't want her *dead!*"

"Honey, what do you think 'the big bang' is?"

"I just wanted to do things like have her new car towed to the junkyard and crushed, big stupid, stupid things like that. Not fucking *murder!*"

Bark sat there and pulled a sandwich wrapped in wax paper out of my duffel bag, unwrapped it, took a bite. While he was chewing and looking at the floor, he said, "Well, then, I got a funny feeling this was all just a slight misunderstanding." He looked up at me and swallowed. "No hard feelings?"

"No hard feelings! I got a tough deal because all the cops had to do was pinch you and you sang. Sang all kinda yellow songs I never heard before." I pulled my neckline down and showed him my bruised and mangled breasts. "And I'm not here a week and I've already almost lost my tits, you fucker!"

He held up his palm so he wouldn't see. "Well there are worse places, you know."

We just sat there looking at each other, me feeling my feelings burning through my arms and legs.

"You didn't really kill her, did you?" Bark asked. "I mean, I know all the evidence points to you, but I just don't take you for a killer. Swear to god."

"No, I didn't fucking kill her."

"Okay, look, I believe you. I thought they had me, because some guy walking his dogs saw a person in a black mask kidnap her in my car, and although they assumed it was a woman they could just as easily remember it as a man if questioned the right way. And the person that saw you throw what apparently looked like a body over the cliffs got my tag number, so everything seemed to be pointing directly at me—"

"—what witness! You know, I thought I just may have blacked out and gone crazy, and yeah, maybe I thought I had thrown her over the cliff, but they don't have a damn body! I can't shot-put a six-foot woman far enough past the rocks to make the sharks eat her."

"Well, you've got a witness and that's your problem. They already sprayed Luminol in my car and found her blood. They're not giving it back to me yet. I dare say, I'm just a little irritated myself, missy."

"She got a bloody nose when I gave her those whip-its."

"Whatever. Listen, I'm just not going to hang my ass out to dry over some goddamned turkey baster drama, that's for sure. If I'd known the cops had a log of checking up on you on Route 1, I wouldn't have given 'em anything, but I didn't even have an alibi. In my line of work, I can't fuck around. You should've told me what you were doing. I thought you knew the other stuff, I uh, sometimes do, and tried to put my ass in the sling because of it, and wanted to save a few bucks from actually having me do the job."

"I'm dead," I muttered to myself. "I'm so dead."

"Look, don't worry about that now. Just get comfortable and I'll try and help you out. I'll stay in San Francisco and take care of your little Nena kitty."

"Why would you try and help me out? You ain't tryin' to pull a fast one on me, are you? Because I don't like fast ones."

"Yeah, you can always find the quick ones in jail."

"I've been framed, I tell ya, I didn't do it."

"Yeah, well, I happen to believe you. That's why I'm gonna help you out. I think you got a bad rap; besides I want my Lexus back so I can blow town. I'm a long ways from home."

"Hey, Flam?"

"Yeah?"

"Why are we talkin' this way?"

"I don't know."

"Yeah, me neither. It's probably this place."

"This is a liberal do-good place. A decent new place where they're trying to save your souls. You oughta be thankful to all the bleeding hearts who voted for this kind of stuff, because you just never know. . ."

"Yeah," I agreed and looked around at the chairs that molded to a behind. "A place of compassion."

"Aaah, I don't know about all *that*. Compassion. . . " Bark nodded and looked wistfully past me into one of his pornographic memories and pointed at me, "Real compassion is when someone sips a cool drink before they give you a blow job." Then he snapped his mind back to the here and now and stood up. "Yeah, well," Bark wrapped the half-eaten sandwich back up and put it back in my duffel bag. "I've gotta scram. I'll leave your clothes with the guard to go through. You can have the rest of the sandwich and I'll go take care of your cat."

If Nena kitty were human, the authorities would've taken her away and put her in a foster home.

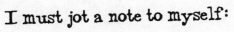
I must jot a note to myself:

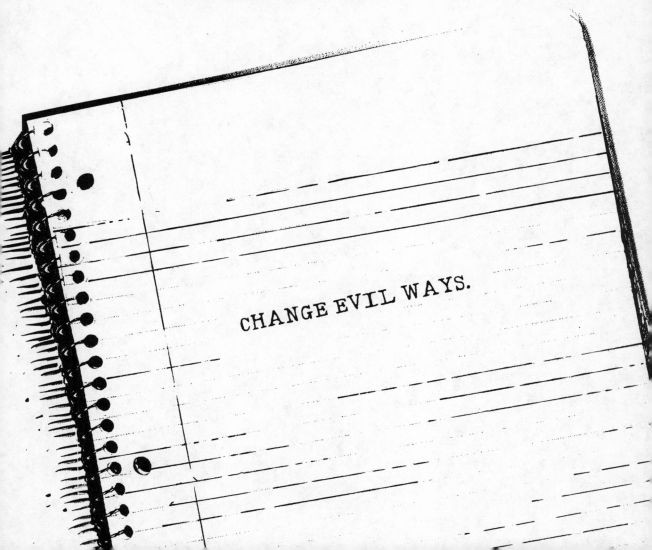
CHANGE EVIL WAYS.

KEEP your Fingers Above
the Sheets, girls. We only
Get to wash them Once a week

|||| |||| ||||

|||| ||||

|||| |||| ||||

|||| ||||

|||

The novelty of prison life wore off with the hydrochloric acid of time and every single day was the same in prison. Without wanting to, I'd cultivated my own New York kind of prison ennui. It was hard not to because most of the women in prison were more stupid than even myself, with them constantly talking big about all sorts of big plans like how to really get someone back this time and how it was someone else's fault. Always someone else's fault.

I vowed never to complain again. Well, I could fake complain, but never for real.

Between the big talkers and the born-again Christians locked up with me, I wished for political unrest on the outside and a sudden influx of political prisoners I could learn things from, get inspired by.

They cut up frankfurters, peel the bananas, and boil the carrots. It's a brutal place, I tell you, and the only penetration comes from the counselors asking all about your past. If getting out of prison is like going to heaven, going to the counseling sessions is like going to first communion class. They try to teach you to say please, thank you, no hitting. The big love of my life had become a spider in a little web at the top of my bunk. Prison doesn't do much for the imagination, so I called her Charlotte. Imagine that. I loved Charlotte and she was sweet. She talked to me now that my guardian angel, Chiquita, had abandoned me now that I couldn't afford to buy her pricey cars and fruit headdresses. **Women.**

But Charlotte loved her name and sometimes she asked me to be quiet because she said I chattered on too much and she just wanted to think. And when she was in that mood, I went back out into the common area just outside and watched a little TV or asked some girl who she was gonna get revenge on when she got out.

But between Charlotte the Spider occasionally needing her space and the monotony of a day just broken up by the rotation of chores, my life and bad movies were starting to crisscross like a schoolgirl's eyes.

Every time I walked down the hallway, I expected to see big black girls, Pam Grier and Cleopatra Jones, rounding the corner with shaky tits and steady guns.

I wanted it to be more dramatic around prison, I just didn't want it to be like *Ilsa the Wicked Warden*.

Ilsa the Wicked Warden had lips long and fleshy like frosty-white painted livers. Her hair was country-singer big and her tits were even bigger and sang even louder. Nothing about her invited you to sit on her lap so she could read you a story in her scary "European" accent, reminiscent of a Nazi who's run away to South America.

No.

She squinted her eyes like target practice, and everything about her whispered in your ear, psst . . . #10, you don't want to play with me? I will maul you when I feel like it. Forget your name. You are #10, and if you ever answer to your name, I will tattoo your number on your breasts. But if I'm pleased with you, I may give you a nickname. Your own special nickname. Maybe I'll call you #14.

Now, take off your prison uniform so I can beat you and see the welts . . .

And later on a group of savage girls with bad complexions and ten-year-old fashions would be tearing at my flesh by the end of this story as if I were a warm mango.

So one day the nun, Sister May, pulled me by the elbow down a wet hallway that seemed that way naturally. It was like the lowest rung of the inferno. There was no carpeting here. It was dark, and the echo of generators and machines hummed all along the corridor like a monster heartbeat.

Sister May didn't even seem to notice we'd entered the zucchini version of the South Bronx, so I didn't say anything out of respect, in the same way you don't go over to someone's house and say "gross" when you find greasy lipstick on a clean glass.

Actually, Sister May seemed rather perky for a nun that day and I wanted to see if I could accuse her of something heinous and make her blush. Said she had an appointment for me. I thought maybe I was on my way to a special hearing test, the kind that they used to pull you out of class for in grade school, but when I saw a burly muscle-to-fat man in a gray uniform with an embroidered cursive "Bill" over his left breast pocket, I knew nothing good could come of this little walk in the rain because he held a mop in his hand and I hated to clean so much, I would've rather spent a week in purgatory with a bunch of Chihuahuas and a doorbell ringing over and over and over again.

"Tomato, meet Bill," my nun friend said. "He's our janitor and audiovisual man. You'll be doing your work detail with him in the audiovisual department. Running the projector on our weekly movies, and things like that. I thought this would be a nice creative surprise since your file says you worked as an artist on the outside.

"So, say hi to Bill."

"Hi, Bill." Out of habit I extended my hand and he just slid his to the top of the mop and nodded: *hey.*

She went on to tell me that Bill set up the projectors and slide shows for special events like "English comedy night" and then he also cleaned up afterwards.

Where are his teeth? I asked myself. A smoldering Chesterfield dangled from Janitor Bill's wrinkled lower lip, thick with spit. The butt was wet and yellow and would eventually burn past his lips, but he wouldn't care. He wouldn't care because his name was Bill.

My experiences with people named Bill have never been real good. Most of the Bills I've known look like they have enemies buried in their flour canisters because they're usually running a few cents short of a dollar, a few sandwiches short of a picnic, their elevators never reach the top floors, they're a scoop short of a pint . . .

. . . While I was trying to come up with more metaphors about guys named Bill, he stood up and slammed my head against a steel door. It didn't hurt as much as I would've thought it would if someone told me they just got their head slammed against a steel door. I was actually surprised at how it was just like being punched with a very, very hard pillow and it quieted me down.

But getting hurt is never as bad as it looks. Sometimes it even feels a little good if you can luxuriate in it, like being sick in bed where you're not responsible for anything because you're not up to being in charge. But if you get the shit kicked out of you and have to pick the kids up from school and go home to fry up some pork chops, I imagine it'd be hard to get into.

I reacted in what felt like a few days, and I slipped on the film of grease on the floor and from another dimension I heard, *what's that about my name?*

Sorry, sorry, sorry I think I said and I scampered away from him on the floor. I really was losing it because I didn't think I'd said anything out loud. Maybe I really was going insane.

The nun told Bill to stop it. She was stuttering, *sh-sh-she d-d-didn't mean it. Why d-d-don't you let her go into the bathroom and get c-c-cleaned up? She's b-b-b-bleeding.*

I didn't know the nun lady was still there, but I looked around and she looked so black and white and holy standing back behind me. She looked liked something had snapped a little. She no longer looked like she'd know what to do in case of a flood: her eyes were wide and frightened, and she walked toward me and reached out her hand with a sympathy that made me break into tears so she'd give me more. I didn't hurt, it all just took me by surprise, and I wanted her to treat me like a sweet little girl.

I took her shaky hand and pushed myself up with a palm on the floor. It was cold, wet, and greasy like it'd been mopped with chicken skins.

H-h-here, here, she forced out. She patted me on the back and walked me to a large private baby blue tiled bathroom. Only hanging from two or three hooks, the plastic white shower curtain was drawn to one side and a short, stiff hose was attached to the tub faucet.

S-s-sit on the edge and clean yourself off, she said.

Thank you, thank you, I cried and now my eyes were fuzzy like they too were covered in chicken-skin grease. She closed the door behind her and I stepped into the cold tub and sat on the edge.

I had never seen a private bathroom in this place and it wasn't near any offices. In fact it seemed like this corridor was closed off. It was dimly lit and the few windows were Plexiglas that was so scratched up and foggy, they also looked like they were covered in chicken-skin grease.

I turned the hot-water knob, and added a little cool water to quiet it down. I pointed the hose at my wrist and it felt like a million terrible years since I'd felt water run over my wrist like a lover's warm tongue that felt wonderfully sorry for me.

I bowed my head and let the water cover me and make my hair small. The cut in my hair stung like seltzer water. There was going to be a large knot later. Getting hurt is always worse later.

I reached for a bar of green soap that had a smaller bar stuck on top so it looked like a fried egg or a Ford Taurus and I smelled something sweet. A cologne I'd probably smelled in an old man's closet before. Cologne mixed with onion sweat and too many packs of cigarettes between an occasional load of wash. In the small bathroom the stench was evil, like a lie trying to cover something bad up.

I turned around and Bill smiled at me. I heard a *click* like a latch, like a lock, like the *snap* of fingers reminding you of something./Something like you've been set up as a paper duck and you're going to go down because of a guy named Bill, a goddamned guy named Bill. I held the small hose of water between my knees pretending it was my loaded gun.

Bill walked toward me faster than I would've liked. He didn't know about the boundaries of America where you don't sit right next to someone on an empty bus. I stood up and pointed the hose at him but it came off the spout and in the end I had to smack him across the face with it. He grabbed at his black billy club—and in my mind I wondered *why does a janitor have a billy club?*—And I dropped the hose and to my knees in the tub because there was nothing else to do.

There you go, Bill laughed.

Get the fuck away from me, I hissed. *I've got diseases they don't even have names for yet.*

Nice try. I already looked you up.

And he grabbed me by the hair and lifted me out of the tub and I stepped back onto the cement bathroom floor. He pushed my head down until I was on my knees in front of him and he lightly tapped the club against my ear and told me I was a whore and knew what to do, so I grabbed his hips, and bashed his crotch against my head and pushed him against the bathroom door, got to my feet, and kicked whatever I could. I don't remember what, I just remember thinking, *fuck, he's against the goddamned motherfuckin' door and I can't get out.*

I saw the billy club behind the toilet and when I crouched down to grab it, he kicked at my legs and I fell.

Bill crashed down and knocked the breath out of me. I was tired, the wind was out of me and it wasn't anything like before when bending arms behind backs was as easy as green twigs.

He never said anything, he just pressed me into the concrete over and over with crashing waves of nausea, and cut between my legs until they were foreign countries. His sweaty forehead was in my face, so I turned my head up and looked at the different shades of crusty brown streaks on the edge of the tub until I could barely exhale. I just relaxed and smelled him until I thought I would throw up and choke on the contents of my stomach like a rock star. The faster he breathed, the more I could hear the stuff flapping in his nose and I hoped it wouldn't break loose and blow out onto me.

I was so flat I could barely feel him poke at me between my legs. If he was *going* to fuck me I wanted him to fuck me through my underwear so it would be like he may be *in* me but he's not *touching* me.

0-0177-0

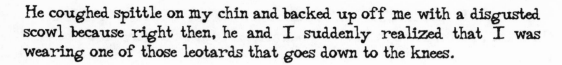

He coughed spittle on my chin and backed up off me with a disgusted scowl because right then, he and I suddenly realized that I was wearing one of those leotards that goes down to the knees.

I started to laugh a little, because I was fading out again. He didn't know it, but I was about to get away. In a moment of two-year-old logic, I knew if I closed my eyes, if I couldn't see him, I knew he couldn't find me.

I started to get up, but my legs felt like rubber from trying to close them the whole time, and I wiped my chin with my shirt and looked up at him as if to say, "sorry Charlie" even though his name was Bill. He fumbled around his belt and came up with a box cutter and I scampered around the floor on three limbs, away from him like a big spider holding out its arm, going, "wait, wait, wait . . . "

Janitor Bill reached out and grabbed a handful of Lycra over my abdomen and yanked me up off the floor, slashed at the fabric around my stomach, and one leg quietly pulled away like a bad run in a dollar pair of nylons.

Standing there with one leg in shreds and the triangle of crushed pubic hair without any U.S. Borders I just knew there was no way, no way, no *fucking* way this could be over like I was a goddamn UPS box to be torn open.

And just in case you were wondering about that exposé you saw on
the news last night, angels are real. The spirits of Mary Magdalene,
Ivana Trump, and Jackie Onassis worked through me like three
rivers joining together to seduce the gay, the blind, the castrated, the
celibate, the uninterested, the dead. So I took a deep breath and
slowly looked up from my vulnerability, flashed him my most
seductive look from my makeup kit, and blew him a kiss.

It was in that momentary wave of confusion that came across his
face that I took a giant step toward him and got my hand on his
zipper, and with the wink of my nose, his pants were down around
his feet and I'm telling him sweet nothings about liking being
played with a little roughly, anyway, but now everything was
okay. To relax. To let me take care of all the grocery shopping. To
sit back because daddy's had a hard day at the office.

I dropped to my knees and tickled the tips of my fingers down the
back of his legs, then wedged my fingers up under his tool belt,
around the elastic band of his yellowing BVDs and slowly trickled
them down to his ankles and tried not to notice the inevitable skid
marks.

"Wow, Bill, very nice. You know, Bill, I just happen to know nice
dicks because, I used to make dicks. Did you know that, Bill?"

Bill leaned against the doorjamb, closed his eyes, and his head bobbed
back on his neck like a backwards nod.

"I've got to move your tool belt around . . ." I whispered. If a banana slug could open its eyes, well then, Bill opened his eyes like a banana slug and I insisted, "Oh, no . . . Let me." And I fumbled with his tool belt for a few seconds so his hammer was just out of reach.

I traced my fingers back down the sides of his furry legs and I noticed a few bald spots, and no hair below the crew-sock level.

I spit on my hand the way my cousin did it through the keyhole. I spit without question, without apology, as if I'd done this a thousand times before and given hand jobs to pay tolls, to pay college tuition, to pay my rent. Truth is, I'd never done it before. Women's magazines call it the lost art. I tightly wrapped my fingers around him and brought my hand up and down like they do all through the John Wayne movies.

Bill's eyes snapped open, and I said, "Now I'm gonna put it in my mouth, okay?"

He snorted an okay, and the thing that was flapping in his nose blew out and to this day, I still don't know where it went. His eyelids just fluttered a little and his head fell back again and I had the entire house to myself again.

0-0180-0

He got a little wet like a girl, and I rubbed the tip of our friend Bill between my thumb and forefinger and

There was the inappropriate/incongruous rusty squeal of something metal clicking . . .

. . . Bill's eyes flapping back open to the vision of me holding a pair of old rusty tin snips in one hand, open and poised a few inches away from the tip of his penis in my other.

"Now looky here, Mr. Boy, it's all up to you."(snap)I smiled, "an easy Sunday afternoon or a rough Monday morning. (click, click) What'll it be?"

(click click click click)

His eyes fluttered a few times before they rolled back in his head, his penis twitched and spit as he starting falling over me. Yeah. That's the last thing I remember before he fell, cracked my neck, and the lights went out in Georgia.

O-018

★ SLICED ★

ZUCCHINI

M a t t r e s s. I'm finally waking up on a mattress. My spine isn't jackknifing like a tractor trailer. Don't even care that I either can't move my arms and legs, or won't. Head feels dense. Heavy. Like duck duck goose and that's all I can really think of. Tap, tap, tap goes the heartbeat so dull, it feels like duck duck goose on my head.

Have I finally gotten so enormous I can't even move or get out of my bed? Is this the day talk shows will come over with their cameras and hoist me into an ambulance so I can weigh myself on a truck scale? And if so, who's been bathing me all this time? How do I get up and go to the bathroom?

I squeezed in my pee muscles and there was that vaguely familiar and horrifying pinch of a catheter. And I remember the thing about the evil janitor.

I want to lift my head up, but it's difficult and my neck's making the sounds of a small child walking on packed snow. Ah, I can still see my toes, so that means I can still wipe myself and this is good, because if you're big enough to make it on to a talk show, you have to have family members sprinkle you off with a little sink hose afterwards. Talk about your unconditional love.

There are big beige cuffs keeping my arms demurely at my sides. Maybe beige so the restraints blend in like more expensive, euphemistic Band-Aids for adults with boo-boos.

I heard the sound of pantyhose walking toward me. My favorite matronly sound. *Swish-swish, swish-swish* the sound of help. The sound of teachers in grade school with cigarette and coffee breath, coming to help me out with my multiplication tables and eventually algebra. Algebra. My least favorite word in the English language next to "guaranteed student loans." And I looked over in the direction of the pantyhose and right there it became a least favorite sound in the moment I saw it was the nun. Sister May. The one who doesn't want you to say "may I?" because she's heard it all before.

"Tomato, you're finally awake." She walked toward my bed and pulled up a plastic chair. The kind of chair that molded itself compassionately to your butt in loud red, and you could throw it against the wall, and it would still mold itself to your butt. Unconditional love.

"How long have I been here?"

"Close to a week." She rubbed my arm. "Listen, I promise to take special care of you, no matter what happens. You have quite a little temper, but I don't think you did any of that on purpose."

With a whole bunch of drugs still wearing off, I was feeling slow and thick. This must've been the infirmary because it was a large white, clean room. White with big windows and bright light like maybe death. Death-white like psychological dreams and tests. Short beds were lined up on either side of me as far as I could see and that wasn't saying much because my contact lenses were dry and sticking

0184-0

to my eyeballs. My mouth was dry, dry like when you get stoned and need ice water to talk and keep your top lip from sticking to your upper gums when you laugh.

"Missing something?" I finally repeated.

"You'll be leaving today, if you'd like."

"No, no, no. I want to stay here forever. I want to rot here."

"You need to talk to me."

"About rotting?"

"No, about what happened."

In spite of who she'd delivered me to, I wanted to be her junkyard dog because that's what I knew you needed to do in here. Become a junkyard dog and not do anything stupid to lose your place in line.

"You know," she started and removed her hand to fold it with the other one in her lap, "you really did a number on him. Bill was really quite a mess."

"Found him?"

"Hmm hmm."

0-0185-0

"You say it like I dumped him into the ocean and you finally found the body."

"No," and she replaced her hand on my arm, "he was right there. I don't think it all looked the way it seemed."

"Sister, please speak plainly with me. I don't know what you're talking about."

"Well . . ." She looked at the floor, took a deep breath and then I remembered Bill was in a bad way.

"Bill's in a bad way," I said.

"Bill's dead," the sister said.

"Yeah, I guess Bill's really in a bad way then."

"You're lucky. You could've been in a bad way, too."

"What do you mean?"

"Well, you're lucky that you only sprained your neck."

"I sprained my neck? Sprained my neck because of a blow job gone bad? That's even harsh by your Catholic standards—don't you think, Sister?"

Sister May blushed and polished her knees with the panache of a little boy mauling his big sister's breasts one night when she comes home real drunk and gives him that one-time-only prehistoric permission that they'll never mention again as long as they live. Never. Ever. Until they're on TV. *Hi, mom!*

"I didn't know you could even sprain your neck," I continued. I had to finally admit to myself that, as darling as this little green place was, riding a motorcycle alongside minivans was turning out to be safer than prison. And if you've ever been in the blind spot of a minivan, which, to its driver is *anything* beyond the screaming pod children, you know that minivans and motorcycles mix like roofies and an honest relationship.

I just felt overwhelmed with how preciously fragile people were becoming all of a sudden. I was killing them like ants and I couldn't seem to help it anymore. And I'd be going to death row or something and they don't even let you wear belts and I can't hang myself oh my God oh my God, higher education and all those student loans for nothing and I broke into sobs. "Oh, Jesus fucking Christ, I didn't kill him, I didn't!"

"No, wait, dear—you didn't kill Bill, he had a heart attack and we found him passed out on top of you and a pair of old rusty tin snips in your hand."

I was glad I'd passed out because, two deaths under my belt, and I still have yet to see a dead body.

"They're not trying to say I caused the heart attack, and am therefore a murderer, are they?"

"No. I told them what happened before I left."

"Yeah . . . uh, why did you leave me with him? I mean, when I got here I half expected some warden to videotape me and another prisoner wrestling in mashed potatoes and then force us into a hot tub afterwards so he could sell the tape to some Mexican porn distributor. . . but *you*, Sister May? Why would you leave me alone with him?"

"Excuse me?"

"Oh, never mind."

And Sister May lit herself a little cigarette and her eyes stared through the wall. "I don't know. It probably has something to do with my mother murdering my father when I was a kid. She found lipstick smeared all over the crotch of his best slacks, and she beat him to death with an iron skillet while she was wearing an armful of charm bracelets . . . I was there. I was about sixteen, and I made all my little brothers stay in their bedroom so they wouldn't see, but I saw the whole thing . . . I just froze. Froze the way I did when Bill lost control. I couldn't stop it.

"That's why I became a nun. I wanted to help people. I wanted to work in a women's prison and help add some humanity..." She looked at me and tipped her ash into one of the water cups. *Tsst.*

"Well, uh, Sister," I said, "I know you were trying to help, but I think you kind of made my situation worse."

Sister May took another drag on her cigarette and said, "I know, I know. But this is why I feel I have a great debt to you while you are here."

After hearing about her mom and what just happened with good old Bill, I wasn't so sure I wanted any more of her help. "The way things are going, I could be here forever ... But why? You're like into God and everything. Shouldn't you be off trying something else, like praying in an Italian convent? Making wine?" I wondered how safe it was being around her.

"I don't know." She clenched her fists. "I just froze." She looked into space, smoking, and trembling just the tiniest bit. And then she shook herself out of it and said, "But that's why I feel I must take it upon myself to help you in any way I can."

"Can you help me escape?" I smiled hopefully, even though if she helped me out, I'd probably get shot in such a way that I'd be paralyzed from the mouth down.

And then she looked at me over her glasses like a teacher in pantyhose who was telling me I knew better, and of course I did.

"Okay, well thanks, for whatever you're going to do." May God be with me.

"My job will be to bring you as much peace as possible from now on. I will take care of you while you're here. I will stand up for you."

"Well, thank you, Sister." May Jesus and Mary be with me, too. And the Archies. The whole gang of the Archies.

She put her cigarette in the plastic water cup and poured some water from a pitcher in and it went *ssst* again.

I went to reach out for the pitcher but I forgot my hands were tied. "Uh, could you take these off?" And I wiggled my fingers.

"Oh, of course," and she did. I slowly eased myself into sitting up and reached for the water. I took the lid off the pitcher and swigged the rest.

"You don't happen to have another cigarette, do you?" I twinkled at her and she lit one for me. "I have a confession I'd like to make."

"A real confession, or is it just a manner of speaking."

"Why, that's a funny question, Sister. I guess just a manner of speaking. I don't wanna pin myself down to anything permanent anymore. You gotta be careful."

"Okay."

And I told her I was thinking about my adolescent crush on a dog named Billy.

Billy was a charming Irish setter and we never looked at each other *that special way* until I was at my aunt's house. One morning she went off to the store with the kids and I must've been eleven.

I got out of the shower, dried and dusted myself with perfumed powder, then pranced around the house naked because it was like a decadent luxury. I stood in front of the mirror in my aunt's room, combing my hair.

It was summertime in the Bronx and I could barely hear street noise below. The sheer white curtains were blowing just enough to look like pregnant stomachs. The air smelled fine. The garbage strike had long since passed, so I felt beautiful and my breasts were hard and brand new but no one ever had to know. I felt like I'd been a woman all my life, explaining the ways of love to circles of little girls on urban rooftops, warning them against feminine deodorant sprays, vinegar and water, and lines like "I promise I'll pull out" or "I feel like I've known you forever," packing cigarettes against my thighs and confidently unpeeling thousands upon thousands of tampons the way others unwrapped Doublemint gum.

Billy must've sensed that I was feeling all woman because he trotted in like a man, like a dog, like a man-dog, and started licking me between the legs without even saying excuse me.

I (obligatorily?) gasped like a virgin at the turn of the century and pushed Billy away, but I was tingling down there like cherry soda.

Billy must've felt like cherry soda too, because he came back at me and his tongue was big and flat, flat and big like the palm of a man's hand. He looked more handsome than ever.

"No, Billy, no," and I backed up until I bumped against my aunt's bed. "This is wrong . . . Don't . . . Stop . . ."

And I thought to myself, Billy, if loving you is wrong, I don't wanna be right.

"Don't . . . Stop . . ." I crawled away from his nose. "No, don't . . . Stop . . ."

Billy looked at me, beautiful long hair blowing in the summertime wind, the color of chestnuts if you covered them in clear nail polish, and he looked at me like he was kind of unsure. I didn't realize what

I was saying, don't stop, don't stop. It was confusing the dog side of Billy. As a dog he wanted to stop, roll over, and lie down./Good dog./But when I added don't, it reminded him he was also a man-dog who wanted to believe that no meant yes./Bad dog. Bad, bad dog.

I was scared because looking at him and the scandalous desire in his dog eyes, I started to feel like yes and a little red, more like cherry soda and he had to go. I knew nothing about the couplings of girls and dogs, so he had to go because he couldn't even talk me into it. He was a dog, and dogs don't talk.

At least, not with their mouths. Billy talked with his eyes, they whispered Gettysburg Addresses of love, and his eyes sadly said good-bye as he shuffled out of the bedroom. Billy was older than me in dog years, and he couldn't understand that I wasn't ready. Billy, don't be a hero, I wanted to say because I wasn't even ready for a human boy. That would be a little over a couple of years away.

A week after my thirteenth birthday, and I was pissed because I couldn't say I was twelve. He was a twenty-year-old basketball player named Theo, at the University of Massachusetts. He was a tall black man with a tiny penis—and good thing since I still had a little mouth. Today if I heard of a twenty-year-old man having sex with a girl a week after her thirteenth birthday, I think I'd do something that would land me back here for real. No mistaken deaths or lost bodies. He'd be right there bleeding to death from three missing legs. I'd push him to the police in a wheelbarrow and hold out my old-lady wrists.

But I digress. And digress from human sexuality is just what I wanted to do with Billy. Billy and I never had a chance alone quite like that again. After that, Billy would come down and lie at my feet while I'd read passages of *The Exorcist* to him. They weren't real big on books in that house, so other than the Bible, that was the only book I could find. Maybe there's irony in that, but I don't much feel like gouging it out.

I went back to my grandmother's once the summer was over and I had to go back to school. And sometime in the fall, my cousin took Billy out for a walk in the park and Billy was never seen or heard from again. He was kidnapped because of his beauty. I only hoped that it wasn't a man who was attracted to Billy because that gets weird like *diet* cherry soda.

If other girls had extra special feelings toward their pets, they weren't discussing it in the ladies' room. So I've always felt all alone.

Except for once when I was reading *Hustler* magazine, which I often stole from the newsstands during my time of perverse loneliness. In hindsight, now I realize I kept returning to the probably fake letter of a woman getting down on her hands and knees on her day off and having sex with her Doberman. Each time I read it I wanted to stop short of the ending where the dog got too excited, bit her on the ass, and she had to go to the hospital and tell everyone what she did. I didn't want to believe it. So I wouldn't. If a dog's not biting the hand that's feeding him, why the hell would a dog bite the ass that's fucking him? I tell you, it just doesn't add up.

As I grew into a woman, I felt a sadness for losing that one adolescent summer moment where the pregnant curtains were blowing across the New York windows, never knowing what we could've had.

I told her all this because after Bill, the evil janitor, and Hooter, the cheating and thieving carpet-lickin' love of my life, I was seriously thinking of leaving the gladiator games of human sexuality. Go for the kind of love that licks the salt off your hand.

I put my second cigarette out and smiled at Sister May.

She asked me if I, uh, felt better and I nodded yes.

"Wow." I pushed the ashes around with the butt. "What a relief to finally talk about Billy the Irish setter. You know, I've never told anyone about him." Sister May slowly nodded and crossed her legs the other way. I was leaving her a moment to be a part of the conversation, maybe admit some of her unusual feelings toward animals. Rare enough to be pink. But she didn't say anything, just kept looking at the tiles on the floor, so I kept on going. "Well, now do you want me to tell you about what happened back there with Bill the janitor audiovisual guy?"

0-0195-0

Sister May wiggled around in her butt-cupping seat a little bit and cleared her throat. "Perhaps we can wait for another time?" She smiled at me hopefully and patted me on the hand.

"Sure, of course." I smiled. "I feel I have a weight lifted from my shoulders."

Sister May stood up and said I should get even more rest and she'd be in to bring me some supper later. Then she walked out the door.

See, there's just *something* about that name Bill.

0-0196-0
0-0196-0
0-0196-0

In the week or ~~two~~ two that followed, Sister May kept true to her promise to take good care of me. She brought me dinner and had the new janitor guy bring me another foam mattress since Big Bob had never given mine back. That night I wanted to go back because there was no TV in the infirmary and since no one was there, it felt lonely with all the rows of beds and the sun going down. I'd rather have Big Bob Zadora twist my titties into balloon poodles or airplanes and wear them on her head.

But when I left the infirmary to go back to my cell in the tank, Big Bob had returned my mattress and had made my bed. Made my bed.

"Whoa, what's this?" I asked her. All three girls were reading books on their bunks.

They all sat up when they heard my voice and smiled at me. Big Bob said, "Well, after all you did, I figure you deserve a lot of respect."

"Wait, wait, wait. What do you mean 'after all you did'? How do you know what happened?" I put the mattress I was carrying against the wall and looked at her suspiciously. "Did you pee on it or something?" I leaned over and sniffed my bed.

"Noooo. There's nothing to do around here, so word spreads fast like a gasoline fire, and after what you did to that guy, I didn't want you getting too, too pissed off at me."

"Pardon the pun?"

"What?"

"Oh, nothing."

"Well, we're all in here 'cause we're a little crazy you know, but I'm not *that* crazy." She laughed and held out her hand.

I stepped back and held the new foam mattress against me because I wasn't *that* crazy, either.

"Hey, I'm tryin' to shake your hand, bitch."

"Bitch? How can you be a black girl and call me bitch when you're trying to be my friend? Bitch is a fightin' word and girls have lost arm fat for less. You can call me Mad Dog." I made a lot of phony fanfare in throwing the foam back against the cement-block wall and went up to her and shook her hand.

She shook it back hard, like she was one of the ten girls who knew how to shotgun snot onto the sidewalk. "Aw, you know I mean bitch in a friendly way," Big Bob said.

"Yeah, friendly like dyke or nigger. I hate that word, so don't go calling me nigger to try and make me feel good."

"We've got to take back those words, take the power out of 'em."

0-0199-0

"Blah blah blah, I got your power right here," and I squeezed my crotch like an Italian taxi driver.

One of the other girls sat up and asked me what happened, and her girlfriend on the top bunk said, yeah, tell us what happened.

"Well, what did you hear?" I asked as I sat on my bed.

"We heard you killed the motherfucker." Big Bob laughed.

"You're insane, Miss Big Bob." I stuck my head out from under the bunk and leered at her. "That's not funny and I didn't kill him. He had a heart attack. Besides, I don't remember much after a certain point because I passed out. At least that's what they say. That's how they found me."

The wanna-be black girl on the top bunk jumped down and sat down on the floor and hugged her knees. "Well, so what happened?"

"Look you all, I just want to tell you that whatever you've heard, I never killed my ex-girlfriend—"

"—What? We didn't hear that." The wanna-be girl on the floor started laughing.

"Oh, never mind then."

"No, no, no, you can't let that drop now. Finish it," the wanna-be girl on the floor insisted.

"They say I killed my girlfriend, but how can you concede to such a hideous crime when they can't find the body and you can't even remember anything?"

The wanna-be girl said, "Easy. Are there witnesses?"

I looked at the floor. "Apparently so."

"Well, then, there you have it. Witnesses."

"But I don't know who."

"Well usually witnesses to anything want to stay safe as long as possible, so you won't know until the trial what they look like."

"Damn." Big Bob slapped her knee. "If I'd known that, I never would've fucked with you."

"I used to love her, but I didn't kill her. I'm not like you all."

Big Bob leaned over the edge of her bed and said, "Whoa, I get the pun! 'Pissed!' I get it, Sweet Thing."

"Call me Mad Dog." I said all dignified and shit.

0-0201

"Yeah, yeah, yeah. Well, uh, *Mad Dog*, this place is full of innocent people," the baby chick on the bunk smirked.

"No, no, it's true. If I'm gonna tell you this story, you've gotta believe me."

"*Mija*—after that janitor, you're like a goddamn black widow."

"And you talk like you're in a prison movie, you moth-eaten whore."

"Fuck you, Princess."

"Yeah, fuck you, too. And don't call me princess unless you can roll your r's."

"Princess! Princess! Princess!" Big Bob yelled at the ceiling without rolling her r's.

"Hey!" yelled the wanna-be girl on the floor, "tell the goddamn story!"

"Okay, okay. But first." I looked up at Big Bob. "Tell me where you got a name like Big Bob. What's your real name?"

"None of your goddamn business." She crossed her arms and the upper parts spread like bat wings.

"I'm gonna find out."

The other girls yelled for me to tell the goddamn story.

"No wait, I should take this mattress back to Sister May since I don't need it." And I grabbed it and turned toward the door.

"No, no, no!" The wanna-be girl on the floor jumped up and grabbed it away from me. "We can use this when we have our tree-trimming parties," she said in a low voice and jammed it under her bunk.

"Tree-trimming parties?"

They all laughed.

"Yes, " she winked. "They're less about trees and more about trim. Gettin' some *trim.*"

"Oh, no, it's not some kind of weird prison lesbian thing, is it?"

"Oh we're not gay," the baby chick on the bottom bunk giggled.

"We only like to play house when we're in here." The wanna-be girl laughed and waved her hand. "Well, except for Big Bob over here."

"No." I shook my head at the floor. "No, I don't want to be a part of any lesbian reindeer games." I stretched and yawned. "Why don't you all do something normal, like bang metal cups against bars or carve guns out of soap?"

"Girl parties are normal." The baby chick on the bottom bunk looked at me as if I were lost. And she went on to talk about wanking yourself in prison and some girl comes over to help you out. "It's not like you're loggin' in the lesbian hours or anything," she told me. "She's just helping you out 'cause she's got a guy named Billy waiting for her on the outside."

Baby Chick was right. Sometimes it just comes down to a friend helping another friend out. I remembered the time my friend Misty and I were kids and stole a couple of vibrators from a novelty shop in the mall. When we got to her house we ran into her bathroom and still in my winter coat, I dropped my pants and stood against the sink and I let her stick the bigger one inside me so she'd be impressed. She turned it on and when I didn't instantly scream and wave my arms in the air like in the movies, we were both very disappointed.

We tried it another time in her room, but when her mom came in, I snapped my legs shut and pulled the covers over me. We tried to talk loud enough so her mom wouldn't hear the buzzing sound which was more deafening than any tell-tale heart. "Well, thank you, but no," I shook my head at Baby Chick, "Grown-up lesbian stuff's bad enough on the outside. I can't imagine what it'd be like once you add even *more* spontaneous hostility."

"Oh yes you can, Princess," Big Bob bit her teeth at me.

0204-0

"Oh, no, no, no. See, I never knew what I was doing the first time."

And I told them that even though I didn't kill him, I wasn't sorry he was dead and I told them everything. I told them it was a little ditty with all the predictability of a disco song.

The next morning I sat in the cafeteria with my three new friends, and I looked at the wanna-be black girl because I was more curious about her than the baby chick.

"What's your name, anyway?" I asked her.

"Snake."

"Is your last 'Pit'?" I smiled, pleased with myself.

She scrunched up her nose and tilted her head, "Snake Pit?"

"Yeah."

"No." She shook her head. "I don't get it."

"As in 'arm.' "

"Arm?"

"Yeah. Arm Pit." Talk about your being dropped from a balcony. "Never mind."

"Well, no my name's not Pit and it's not Arm, either."

("Where did they get this one?" I nudged Big Bob. She just kept eating and reading the *TV Guide.*)

"Hey!" Snake sat straight up. "Are you making fun of me?"

"Well, you don't know what a snake pit is?"

"Is it like an arm pit?"

"No, no, no. Never mind. Why is your name Snake?"

"My parents were hippies and they named us all after animals. I have a brother named Rabbit and a sister named Moon."

Now it was my turn to scrunch up my nose and turn my head sideways, "But Moon isn't an animal."

Snake sat back in her chair and folded her arms. "You think you're so damn smart then why are you here?"

Snake was absolutely right. Turns out her sister, Moon, had the middle name Gazelle. And turns out that Snake wanted to be a black girl so she could rebel. When you've got hippie parents, the only other outlet is to go clean cut, and that's boring.

Only thing left to do after that is to make fun of how people dance. And that's just downright mean.

Baby Chick next to Snake had that skittish, beat-up way about her that afternoon, so I figured I wouldn't ask her her name. Just keep calling her Baby Chick. Anyway, she was one of those girls who usually looked like she'd been swung around the kitchen a few too many times, crashing her little baby-chick head against particleboard kitchen cabinets.

Things keep happening to little kids that I didn't even think living things could make it through. I mean, you can only throw a dog in front of a speeding truck so many times, for God's sake.

Turns out the reason she woke up crying every night with nightmares, was because she saw her sister get hit by a train while she was looking for frogs.

I'd forgotten a lot of the stories because I just had to move on and pretend I'd never seen any of it because while there are a few laughs, it's a depressing world where dreams are a joke and skinned brutality's okay.

Sister May walked up to us and sat down with a thick envelope in her hands.

"You know," she said to me, "you're getting to be quite famous."

"Ha! I told you guys I didn't belong here." I snorted. "I'm a famous artist."

"Well," Sister May shook the envelope, "you're famous because you are here." And she pulled out a handful of news clippings.

They were clippings of editorials from all over the United States saying I was right for killing a cheating woman. "But I didn't kill her," I said to the clippings and shook them by the shoulders.

Basically I gathered that in the last week, I'd become some sort of cult figure and the repeating slogan was CHEAT AND DIE.

Cheat and die? "Oh my God. They're going to hang me. I've got to be guilty with press like this."

Who the hell had done this? We all burrowed into the clippings, reading for the gist. The gist was the same cheat and die crap that could only happen with a press kit.

I noticed a few different quotes of friends they'd quickly interviewed, but over and over again, I noticed there was always a clean, rehearsed quote from the director of my gallery in New York. They were trying to bank on my little legal problem because they figured I'd sell more fake penises that way.

It was almost better than having me die and the value of my work going up.

I broke into tears and started to cry.

"Well, wait." Sister May pulled out another handful of letters bound in a rubber band. "Maybe this will make you feel better."

I dropped the bundle of mail onto my plate of scrambled eggs and cried some more. The other girls continued to read the articles and eat their own eggs.

Sister May stroked my hair and told me she got me a job working with her on the telephones.

"The telephones?" I lifted my head up and blew my nose.

"Princess, working on the telephones is *the shit*—ooh, sorry, Sister."

"That's okay, Ti'—uh, I mean, Big Bob."

I noticed that slip of Big Bob's name and I cheered up for a minute. "Hey, hey, what did you almost call her?"

A look passed between the two of them, Big Bob's look saying *don't* and Sister May's look saying *sorry, I won't*, and Sister May ignored me and said, "Well, Big Bob, why don't you come work the phones, too."

"Well, what're the phones?" I asked again.

And they explained how some companies contracted some of the prisons to answer the phones for their mail-order businesses. "AT&T does it all the time," she explained. "Like we were some of the ones who've called up Americans, threatening them to switch back to AT&T."

"Or else you'd make them come to a tree-trimming party," I said.

Sister May got up to leave and told us to report to her at twelve in the afternoon.

"Yeah!" Big Bob Zadora hollered, and then she picked the bundle of letters off the eggs and turned to me, "Hey Princess, can I have your eggs?"

"If you keep calling me Princess, I will have to kill you. I really will. And I'm not kidding."

"Fine, can I have your eggs?"

"Sure," I said and pushed them to her.

"Thanks, Princess."

"I told you. I'll give you one more chance, and then I'm stabbing you with my fork."

"Oh yeah, sorry, Princess."

"Stabbing you with this spoon will hurt even more . . ."

You could call us late for Sister May but you couldn't call us late for lunch since we never left the cafeteria.

"You're such a snatch," I informed Big Bob Zadora.

"You're such a leaky paper bag whore."

"Yeah, well you still got your daddy's sperm drippin' down your leg."

I even grossed myself out with that one.

Big Bob and I called each other names like every other sentence just in case the other forgot, and we only stopped when we made ourselves retch just a little bit. When you're in prison, you've got to up the ante, because the same old roller-coaster rides don't scare you anymore.

It was fun working on the phones with her, and I still had a hard time remembering the other two girls' names we bunked with.

"Big Bob, you tramp, did you ever even know the names of the other two girls we bunk with?"

"No, and I don't want to know, because between my social security number, prison number, and all the other numbers in my head, I can't remember the names of a couple of nervous little girls, when I can just yell *hey, hey you* if I need them. I mean, I live with them. It's not like I'll need to look them up in the phone book. Those two are so into each other, they give new meaning to tongue-in-cheek."

And then snakes and baby chicks were like the background extras for my little life story and I forgot about it.

"Oh. Okay."

"Flatulent slut."

"Paper bag strumpet."

It was the perfect time to be working the shift because the phones weren't ringing a whole lot. We weren't doing the AT&T gig, because some men's prison actually had that gig. We were handling mail-order calls for a company called B.B. Lean. It was like a gift company that sold novelty stuff, chocolates, comic books, and sports bras.

I had time to read my mail, most of which was from strangers. A few people I knew sent me cards with pretty pictures on the front, and inside telling me how disappointed they were.

One was from my old therapist. She felt like all her work trying to get me to sit and feel the electrical surges of my anger throughout my body was a waste of time and that she was considering quitting the profession because of me. Talk about a guilt trip. She gave me the same guilt trip for giving two-months' notice for leaving her instead of three. Just like a woman./Never enough, never enough.

I threw it in the trash with the rest of my life, and my phone rang. It was a woman whose voice was a raspberry sandpaper that cut through my common sense and left me swimming in milk and Wheaties. She wanted to order a sports bra and I wanted to buy her an ice cream and tell her to sit on my lap, little girl. Sister May had just left for the bathroom with a Bible, so I knew she'd be a while.

"So, uh, what size bra do you need?" I asked my customer in a slightly disguised lecherous tone. And from there, it was fifteen minutes of phone sex with Big Bob next to me making faces and running her hands up and down her calves.

I should've known better about anonymous phone sex. I'd had three bad experiences before.

I used to do the accidental phone thing, where you get a guy on the phone somehow. Maybe he called you, maybe he's a friend of a friend, and before you know it, you're jerkin' off on the phone at 3 A.M. so quiet your roommate across the hall doesn't hear you. I fell in phone-crazy puppy love with a guy who was the son of a friend of my mom's. We had pictures of each other in the family albums at ages two and three. Started talking all through high school, and maybe in my first year of art school I got a VW Bug. We were far apart and swore we were going to get together but he kept canceling visits, I kept canceling visits. Finally I said fuck it and drove up to New England in the middle of the night and got caught in a snowstorm. Took me like thirteen hours, with no heat and a gray-and-red Mexican blanket on my lap. No goddamn heat.

By the time I got there I was miserable and frozen and we didn't know how to be with each other. It was so strange.

See, if this were a novel I would've made that story taste like chocolate where we run into each other's arms, have a couple little sexual tension arguments, and end up doing the tango in a public fountain.

Another time I was working at a job I actually liked and I had to deal with a printer guy 3,000 miles away. I got fired, he tracked me down at home, and a week later he flew out to stay with me for nine days. We had awkward sex the first night to get it over with, and he told me about his childhood, how he used to rub up against dogs when he was in high school (said cats were too squirmy), and then he said he liked blondes, and he said all his friends probably thought he was gay. Could be. Sometimes gay boys and girls end up having sex together for a change of pace that they don't have to explain. Don't ask me to explain.

And another time before that, I think I was about twenty, I met a guy over the phone while I was ordering shoes and he keyed into me somehow. Guess I talk too much and gave so much away, it wasn't hard to pick up on me because he had a southern drawl. A couple weeks after we'd been having phone sex, I get a call just as I'm leaving for work and it's his wife telling me she found my letters, and did I know he was really fifty-five and had five kids? No.

I didn't care as long as he kept talking but the company taped conversations for quality control, and he got fired. I got a broken heart.

So I just didn't really like talking to anonymous people so much anymore. You can't see facial expressions, body language, all those little things that don't make any noise but do make a conversation. When things are anonymous and safe, everyone says all sorts of shit they usually keep to themselves. Then comes that *"Oh my God I can totally be myself with you, I love you, where are you, come here"* shit. But like I said, this girl's voice had me swimming in soggy Wheaties and I forgot everything.

And when Sister May came back in, and I whispered that I had to go, my customer promised she'd call me back with a *firm* color choice same time tomorrow . . . Ooooh. She said *firm*. A shudder went down my spine, just imagining that got blood flowing, circulating, instead of pooling around my ankles again.

It was like cherry soda all over again.

And just in time to save me from Big Bob's remarks making it all go flat, Big Bob's own phone rang and I gave her the finger just as she answered, "Good afternoon, and thank you for calling B.B. Lean. May I take your order?"

Sister May asked how things were going and I said fine. That I had a customer waste fifteen of my minutes and after all that she wasn't sure about the color yet.

"That happens," she said, smiling proudly. "You girls are doing well." She had no idea that I was stuck to the chair like a suction cup.

I leafed through more of my mail, and came upon a postcard with a picture of the California coast. I turned it over and screamed. What I saw there made my blood clot, my eyes go dry, and my heart wait. I screamed bloody murder.

"What is it? What is it?" Sister May rushed over to me and I jammed the postcard in her face. She looked at the picture then read the back with a puzzled look on her face. Big Bob hunkered down in her chair and covered her other ear with her hand and apologized to her customer, but I didn't care because she wasn't dead! She was never dead!

"Look! She's alive! She's alive!"

"Shhh, Tomato, what is it? It doesn't say anything, it just says you're *here*. What are you talking about?" Sister May was pulling me out of the room so Big Bob could finish her call. But I was too busy waving my ass, doing my little she's-alive dance, which is not unlike my "this chicken's good" dance.

-0218-0

I gave Sister May a big kiss and pinched her cheeks. "Of course it says I'm here! Exactly! Exactly! That's exactly why I know she's alive! And I'm not going to hell after all!" I waved the postcard into the penitent sky and kicked my legs up in the forgiving air because neatly printed on the other side was the phrase,

TOMATO WAS HERE.

Now that I knew Hooter had to be alive because someone had seen her derriere, I had hope again, and I had a plan. I would lose a bunch of weight like Oprah and crack walnuts between my butt cheeks, as the *cheat and die* girl, I'd have a press conference where I would come out pulling a wagon full of beef like she did, to show how much weight I'd lost.

I decided to spend some time in the gym that evening. After supper, the girls usually liked to watch television, smoke cigarettes, and talk about the same things they talked about the day before and the day before that, so it was usually quiet then.

As you've probably guessed, the prison gym didn't look like your average butt-thong club where you had to lose weight before you went. The walls were colored in a somber blue-gray to keep prisoners from feeling too energetic or impulsive, as that's what got most of us here in the first place.

Since the prison was new, so was the equipment, and it didn't have that chipped metallic feel, although it had that sweaty smell since there were no windows, no ventilation. The only bright color emanated from the center of the room, where the floor was covered in bright royal blue mats for stretching or doing yoga. On Saturday mornings, there was a yoga class. Four white hippie girls who were in on drugs took that class, but since the prison was full of mostly colored girls, there were only about three of those hippie girls doing the yoga thing.

The rest of the women kept putting requests in for karate or self-defense classes, but like not painting the gym in red or yellow primary colors, the administration apparently thought it was best to stay away from things that teach you how to beat the shit out of someone else.

In one corner there were a couple of rarely used treadmills, a StairMaster, and a rowing machine in another corner. When you're in prison, you don't look as tough using a StairMaster as you do bench pressing even fifty pounds.

The rest of the perimeter was covered with weight benches and racks and racks of weights and shiny chrome bars.

I walked over to the treadmill in front of the mirror bolted to the wall. Since prisoners generally can't be trusted with glass mirrors, as that's how some of us also got here in the first place, it was a plastic mirror and had a touch of a fun house effect. Let's put it this way: it didn't exactly inspire one to dash off and put on a butt thong. I looked half as tall and twice as wide.

So, it wasn't the kind of mirror that made you walk faster, harder, faster on the treadmill. No, it was the kind of mirror that inspired one to crush down on the backs of your sneakers, and shuffle toward insanity and that's just where I wanted to go and talk to a friend. A friend who sort of looked like me, but not really. A special little friend in the wavy plastic mirror. The same special friend who told me to squirrel away sugar packets, free condoms, and toothpicks.

Not the kind of special friend who suggests I keep a mannequin dressed like Mom in the attic or tells me to shoot postal workers. No, no, no. A nice friend who likes free stuff.

"But I don't understand," I said to my fun house friend, "if it wasn't her handwriting on the postcard how do you make out that she's alive?"

I immediately answered so my fun friend wouldn't feel ignored. She was a touchy fun friend: "Because if I threw her in the water, and no one's found the body, I'm the only one who would've known what I wrote on her butt." I started walking on the treadmill because lifting weights reminded me too much of Refrigerator Girl from my first night in.

If this were a novel I'd tell you that I was really running my daily seven miles. I'd pick an odd number because five or ten sounds fake like a cheap store, a cheap lie. I could do some really good thinking while looking at the poster on the wall with every stretching exercise imaginable and imagining them as sexual positions I'd never experience because being limber enough to throw my leg over the back of my bike had been limber enough for me.

"You wrote 'Tomato was here' on her butt? You're one crazy, crazy sonofabitch, you know that?"

"Yeah, well I'm different now. That was then, this is now. She's alive. And don't call me crazy."

"Yeah, well don't you call me crazy, either."

"I didn't."

"Just in case."

"But that still doesn't account for the fact that, as you said, some tourist who actually was crazy might've found her and read what you wrote on her butt and tossed her over the edge."

"Aha, but if they did that, they would've had to pull down her pants to read her butt, then they'd have to throw her over and track me down to this place."

"Sweet pea, you've been in the papers. You're not that hard to track down these days."

"And then how would they've even known there was writing on her butt?" I jumped off the treadmill and stood in front of the mirror with my hands on my insane hips. "Look, I'd have to agree with you more if it weren't for the fact that I pulled her pants up. That's an awful lot for a vicious tourist to do. Pull her pants down, read her butt, throw her into the ocean, and send me taunting postcards."

"Maybe you're right," my fun friend replied.

"I've *got* to be."

"Well, but you haven't answered the main question: then who sent you the fucking card anyway?"

"Maybe she did."

"But it's not her writing."

"Yeah, I don't know about that part, but what I do know is that she's got to be alive. Maybe she's home right now and she told the story to someone and they put two and two together, and they wrote me a postcard. She doesn't even read the newspapers. Maybe she doesn't even know I'm in jail for supposedly murdering her."

"Pea pod, dear . . . I hate to say it, but get real. I think you don't want to admit you fucked someone up."

"Look, I'm not like you. I don't *really* belong here. You just don't get it, do you?"

"Do you know why I'm here?—"

"—No, I don't want to know. I don't want any more of this greasy-chicken-skin place on my skin."

"Don't you want to know who I even am?"

"No, don't tell me shit. I don't want to know. When you get out, you can come stay at my flat, we'll listen to John Denver records, drink a little wine . . . You can tell me all about it when we're not here. I need it this way."

"Pea pod, this isn't about you—"

"—no, I don't want to know. I don't even fucking belong in this place. Things just got a little out of hand for me, that's all."

"Don't you think they're getting a little out of hand right now? You're not talking to little spiders named Charlotte anymore. Sweet pea." She smacked her knee and finally said, "We're all in the clink, the big house, the cooler, because things just got a *little out of hand.* Prisons pop up all over this great land of ours like mushrooms because things just keep getting a *little out of hand.* Get it, my little pea pod of love?

"You belong here just like me. If your Hodie was alive and going to work, someone would've told her she's supposed to be dead and that you're in prison for it. Your friend at your apartment would've seen her. I think this postcard is all just some kind of mean little coincidence. You know, sending you a postcard of the ocean, freedom and all, sending it to jail and writing 'Tomato *was* here.' Get it?"

"No."

"Like Tomato *was* here—in freedom—but she's *not here* any*more.* Understand? Sweet pod, when you do something so bad to somebody, something *so terrible* you can't make it better, it's hard to live with yourself without taking street shit to smooth the edges and make you not think. Sometimes I even feel real bad about kids I used to tease, or money I used to take from people who were helping me out."

"No! That's your delusional guilt. Fuck you, buster. You are so, so wrong, I can't even tell you. But this . . . I know it's true because I can smell it."

"Then go tell your friend, what's his name?—"

"—Bark. Bark Flammers."

"Yeah, well, then tell your friend Bark to see if her lights are on at home, ask around and see if anyone's seen her at work."

"Look miss pod, let's just get real. If she's been moving around, tell him to get some evidence and you should be outa here like that. But I think you're chasing a red fish."

"Red fish?"

"Yeah."

"A red herring?"

"Whatever."

"Red herring. Smelly red fish to put you off your scent."

"Yeah, and by the way, you're starting to smell like a little red herring yourself, my little rotting pea pod. Anyway, you should've written something a little more clever on her butt than, 'Tomato was here.' What kind of stupid shit is that? Now, if you put your pin number on her ass, and got a postcard, you'd know for sure."

"That wasn't the point to put my pin number on her butt."

"Yeah, I guess not, because you're here thinking you're some kind of Nancy Drew that wish-you-were-here postcards are leading to a whole bunch of clues."

"—I'm gonna go find some red *pescado*, see you later."

"Yeah, you do that."

She was right, and I hated her for it. I was pissed that I couldn't just take the postcard to a judge and explain everything. The way she said it, my logic had more holes than a movie star's hand-ripped jeans.

"ALL CATS' FEET SMELL LIKE FRITOS."
---MARK LAMMERS

"Here's your cat. I hate your goddamn cat!" That's the first thing Bark said to me when I met him in the visiting room at the end of the week. No mincing words. Nena kitty was in a little cardboard cat carrier, same color as my arms. He'd put a handmade hair ribbon muzzle on her and she was growling and clawing at the cardboard.

"You know, here you are in prison and your Nena kitty starts acting out. All crazy and shit. You know, that's no mistake. This is exactly how the cycle doesn't get broken."

"What cycle?"

He was talking about the cycle of abuse, neglect, breaking the law. You start and you pass it on down through the line. He said, "For God's sake, break the cycle."

"Bark, she's a goddamned cat. She can't break the law."

"Look!" He put the box down and lifted up his hands and lifted a foot up to his side of the table. His hands looked like they'd been through a paper shredder and his ankle looked like a clump of ground beef was stuck to it.

"Ew, that's gross. Don't show that to me. I'm in prison, I see enough horrors."

"Well, I'm going to kill your goddamned cat. I brought her here to leave her with you, but they won't let her stay. No pets."

"You should put some calendula or aloe on that ankle and it'll heal better."

Bark rolled his eyes. "Herbs are only good if they're sprinkled on little animals in frying pans."

"Yeah, well, whatever. Nena kitty just needs to get used to being alone with you . . . Hey, you're not roughhousin' with her, are you?"

"Oh ho ho! Fuck you, bitch! Everyone's gotta blame the gay guy for all the missing car stereos or every church burning. I'm different now, but speaking of wrestling kitties, I *have* been spending most of my time watching Sumo wrestling for the strongest man in the world contest and I'm newly inspired. They all have big bellies and little necks, but I'd give them *all* kitty baths. Now I want to be big, so big that I talk little and use my flatulence to punctuate my grunts. I'm going to lift weights all week long. I want hands like frying pans, thighs like ham hocks, and arms like pythons—"

"—Okay, okay. I just knew a guy once who admitted he wrestled nude with kitties."

"Yeah, that's sick, because you can't even wrap those black sashes over their privates so they stay on."

"What?"

"Oh, nothing."

"Yeah, well, don't kill her because little murdered feline spirits will follow you. Trust me, I know."

"Nena kitty used to be so content. She frolicked in the cat litter and afterwards cleaned her feet like she was both Jesus and Magdalena. The rest of the day she'd chase the sunspot around the room and sleep in it. Now, look at her. She's gone bad. *Real bad*, see? She thinks my ankles are tiny mice to stalk and kill. I have to run across the floor and jump on the sofa or the bed. And I'm helpless when I'm taking a shit 'cause you've just got that goddamn lesbian curtain for a bathroom door.

"You've really got to take this parenting thing much more seriously than you have been. Now me? I'm not interested in breeding in the typical way. Cloning's where it's at. I'd make another me, a whole family of me at different ages. Become my own parent and see how I turn out without all that baggage. Then I'd leave all my money to me, and if I had sex with myself it wouldn't be pedophilia, it would be masturbating."

I nodded and changed the subject. "So have you, uh, talked to your old partner, Kris, lately?"

And he said yeah, she was doing fine. Bootsy was hell-bent on having a turkey-baster baby and if she didn't find a donor soon, she'd resort to peep-show booth scrapings. Then Bark tells me about

0-0231-

some of the porn movies he's seen lately and he tells me about one
with a big stupid, stupid-looking guy jerking off in a gas station
bathroom and who then slips up and gives the gas station attendant a
blow job. He said I would've really liked that one, and he's probably
right. I like guys accidentally sucking each other's dicks as long as
there aren't modular sofas or dramatic flower arrangements in the
background. Eyeliner fag stuff just doesn't do it for me.

But for the fifth or sixth time in my life, our sexual proclivities
were making me gag so I interrupted. "Yeah, yeah, good," I said. I
wanted to tell him about the anonymous postcard I got, and ask if
he'd check around a little, just see if Hooter was around, answering
the phone or the door. . . Maybe there was some kind of dead Hooter
mistake.

He said that in case I'd forgotten, his car was still impounded. I
told him to rent a car. It probably went a little something like this:

Bark walks up to the counter, looks the young lad behind the
counter in the face and says I'd like a car.

Kid asks for a driver's license and a credit card, and Bark asks *what
for? I'm here, aren't I?*

The whole thing will go that way, with Bark wanting *them* to pay
him to take a huge Town Car, pay for gas and a hot oil massage.

Bark thinks you're supposed to make him happy at your expense, whether or not you're even getting paid. Bark grew up with black cleaning ladies who wet nursed him, so he doesn't know what it's like to serve the public in a warm and friendly way. His service is blowing up cars . . . And stuff.

By the time he's done, the rental kid will probably break into tears, quit, and never work with the public again. Rental kid will probably go work on a wildlife reserve in Africa and shun humans after renting a car to Bark.

"Sure, sure," he said, "yeah, whatever. I'll rent a car if you pay for it." Then he said he had to go shopping and would be giving the guard a box of books for me. Smutty, one-handed books that the girls in my tank could read to each other.

I ended up drawing dirty pictures to go with them.

I was such a *bad, bad* little girl.

Arf, arf.

0-0277
0-0233
0-0233

LESBIAN MISTLETOE

Big Bob Zadora appeared to be correct in the two months that followed, because Bark found no evidence of Hooter being alive.

I started to resign myself to the fact that I'd be here for a very long time, or possibly somewhere way worse after the trial.

Big Bob Zadora, the generic white girls, and I pulled out the extra foam mattress one weekend. We removed all of our mattresses from the bunks and spread them all over the floor. But if I was bad at one-on-one lesbian sex, I was even worse at the lesbian orgy thing. I don't even want to talk about it.

Big Bob Zadora told me to stop what I was doing and she flipped me on my back but I told her to stop, and I got up and read a dirty book while they went on with the whole thing. I just wasn't into it because I don't like fucking people I'm forced to be around afterwards. It's not natural for me and I don't care what anyone says about cuddling and talking about rosy futures and stuff.

The next day, instead of calling me Princess, she started to also call me bottom. She said things like, "Come 'ere, Bottom, I got something to give you. A sex drive."

I just laughed like ha, ha, very funny and I told her I was going to find out her name. "Oooh, no you're not, Princess."

"C'mon." I looked at my watch. "It's almost noon. We've got to go work the phones."

"Oh shit, you're right." And Big Bob jumped up and put on a bra out of respect for Sister May.

I watched her roll up her tits like Ace bandages and carefully set each one in a cup. A bra cup, not a coffee cup. "You know," I started, "there was a cartoon in *Hustler* once where this old lady smashed the rats in her house with her long tits. You've got big, long tits like that . . . Is that how you got in here? Bashing someone across the head with your—" and after she threw me on the floor and twisted my tit until I could whistle, I had to wonder what I was thinking to say this out loud. I really must learn.

We were walking down the hall and I was cupping my tit, making it feel better and trying to protect it from further harm.

"So," Big Bob asked while she strutted through C-section, where all the girls were younger and louder. Mere first-graders. They were in for less time, so they were sloppier and wilder babies with minor infractions, like throwing eggs at old ladies' houses. Those baby girls didn't much care for putting up curtains like those of us who had to do serious hard-boiled time. *Oh, to be a young, plucky thing again,* I thought. Big Bob and I swaggered like two sixth-graders because we were from F-section. We were serious offenders with funny names. "When you have phone sex with that girl—"

"—Veronica."

"Okay, Veronica. Well, when you talk to her, who's in charge?"

"What do you—?"

"—Oh, you know exactly what I mean. I'd assume you were the bottom, only on the phone you sound like you're the one in charge." Big Bob looked at me sarcastically. "I find that so hard to believe."

I punched her in the arm. "Shut your spam hole."

And we passed by C-section's lounge and all the bony white girls whooped and hollered when Big Bob Zadora passed by as if she were the lesbian from Ipanema.

I yelled loudly enough for everyone to hear, "Hey, Big Bob, sorry about that yeast infection," and she punched me in the arm.

Big Bob waved and smiled at them.

I said, "You know, just once, I'd like for some beautiful woman with long hair to come on to me. Some girls want an opposite woman, some want someone who looks exactly like them. That's almost like masturbating. But me, I want a woman who looks the way I *wish* I looked. Glamorous. A girl who doesn't walk into parking meters when someone winks at her." Like me.

"Two femmes?" Big Bob scowled. "That's just not natural."

"Natural?"

"Yeah, there's always gotta be like two different sides in a yin yang kind of thing."

"Yin yang?"

"Yeah, already, now quiet, quiet, we're almost there."

"Well at least you've got respect for church people."

"Sister May's one of those nuns who are really lesbians."

"Whaaaat?"

"You mean you didn't know?"

"No, but now that you mention it, she does remind me of my gym teacher."

"Oh yeah. I knew a lot of lesbians who started off at the convent. Nuns in each other's beds, getting up early to sneak back to their own rooms. It happens all the time."

"All the time?"

"Sure. Who do you think it was who introduced guitar music into mass? Nuns. Now you get it when you realize how much lesbians like that folk music. Folk is in lesbian blood. You can't fight it. Sure, some rebel and go punk, but what are they rebelling against?

Folk. You can rebel against your parents and men in general, but you need them to define what you are and what you're not. Shhh. Come on."

"Wow, you're deep."

"Most lesbians are deep."

And in we went to the phones that knew no man.

So I barely noticed what I was hearing in the background while I was on the phone with Veronica.

But that same Chiquita Banana guardian angel of mine who was there years earlier, banging on the windows of my mind, warning me against shaving my eyebrows into Puerto Rican surprises, was back in my life, after six months in the clink. Now banging and banging again. She was back in a flamboyant flurry of color, trying to tell me, warn me, surprise me . . . I wasn't sure.

"No, no one in my family is named 'Betty.' Yeah, sure. I could look good in blond hair . . . Wait, hold on," I said to Veronica and clicked the hold button.

I sat there with the vague feeling that's like a hair in your mouth. You can't find it, but pull, pull, pull and aim at it like clay pigeons in the sky.

What was it? I heard the faint buzzing of our computers, Sister May was in the other office typing on an old typewriter. The romantic kind that leaves holes in your paper from typing periods.

Big Bob Zadora was taking an order and there was nothing special about the song on the radio in the background.

". . . Okay, ma'am, so that'll be it then? Just a case of Devil Girl chocolates? . . . Okay, and that's in California? Wow, must be some kind of premenstrual event. Well, we'll send that right away.

Thanks for your order then," and Big Bob Zadora hung up the phone.

"Wow," she said, "what a fanatical order."

"Wait, Big Bob," I rolled my chair over to her, looked at the name on the order, didn't recognize it, and tapped my teeth with a pencil. "Is that all they ordered?"

"Betty, aren't you having phone sex with Veronica?"

"Oh yeah," and I rolled back over to my carrel and told Veronica I had to call her back. I turned to Big Bob with my eyes so wide they nearly popped out, "Big Bob, was that a woman who just ordered an *entire* case of Devil Girl chocolate?"

"Yeah?"

"California?"

"Yeah, so?"

"Oh my God . . . Can't be . . . But it's *got* to be."

"What?"

"Big Bob, you slut, you drippy supermarket slut, she *is* alive! I'm telling you, she's out there." And I rolled over and bit her arm fat until our chairs were sliding out underneath us.

"Get offa me! Stop it!"

Crazed by carnal confinement, ripped by prison pigs, torn by penal passion.

I pulled a folded up piece of paper from the inside of my bra and signaled for the visiting-room prison guard as if she were a waitress, to pick up and bring it around to Bark.

It had the name and address of a lady in a small town in California.

"Yeah? What's this about," Bark asked me after reading the address. "Unless it has to do with a big, finger-licking black man's penis, I don't want to hear about it."

"Oh come on come on come on," I whined. And then I pressed my face against the Plexiglas partition and whispered through the salt and pepper holes: "Today Big Bob Zadora got an order for a case of Devil Girl chocolates. A whole case, Bark, *nothing else.*"

He snorted. "So?"

"Well, Devil Girl chocolates, a whole case . . . I think Hooter's alive, Flammers."

"Didn't we go over this something like five or six months ago when you first got here and were just starting to be insane? You were so cute then . . . " Bark sighed dramatically and wistfully. "I remember it like it was yesterday. Little baby steps to insanity, and now you're running . . ."

I slammed my fists up and down on my little counter side. "I'm not kidding, you asshole, listen to me."

He sat straighter and looked at the paper more seriously this time.
"But this isn't her name, and you said she never left San Francisco
proper for anything."

"Well, she never did before, but . . ." I plopped back into my vinyl
office chair with the wet spine of lost hope.

"Okay, okay. You goddamned lesbians just suck the life out of me,
you know that? What the hell's in it for me? Haven't you just done
enough, missy?"

"Oh come on, please? Just drive down there and check it out."

"I can't. They still won't release my car, you bad, evil person.
They say it's evidence."

"Rent another car."

"Oh, no fucking way. After the hassle with the last rental company,
I can't go back to them."

"There are others, use another one."

"I hate those people. They're morons. Absolute morons."

"Bark, I'm desperate."

"I'm not going on another one of your insane wild goose chases, darling. I don't mind visiting you the way others visit their parents in convalescent homes once a week, but I've got to get on with my life."

"Come on, you're staying in my house, what more do you want?"

"Yeah, and your cat's going to make me a goddamned amputee. I've already lost my foreskin. What more do *you* want?"

"Well, just take my motorcycle, then. Take a sandwich with you. Some lemonade. Turn it into a nice little afternoon adventure."

"Uh, excuse me! Knock, knock! Is anybody home in that little scary mind of yours? Darling, there is absolutely nothing adventurous about looking for a lesbian when all I want to do is give a kitty bath to some big black man since I'm not running across very many Sumo wrestlers in California."

"Look, I've gotta go. Our time's up. Just please . . . The keys are inside my motorcycle jacket and that's hanging next to the front doo—"

"—yeah, yeah, yeah, I know where they are, but you seem to forget I don't remember how to ride a goddamned bike, missy."

-0246-0

"Just rent a car," I begged. "Just rent a car and check it out. If it's her, all I need is for you to bring her back and prove she's alive. That's all."

"Wait, wait, wait—bring her back? How am I supposed **to do that?** What if she won't come back?"

"Make her come back. Or at least hold up a current newspaper in front of her and take a picture the way kidnappers do on TV."

The guards came **in**, and I got up to go.

"Okay," Bark said, "but you owe me big, missy. Big, I tell ya. When you get out of here, I want a large black man in my bed, waiting for me and all lathered up with peanut butter."

"Yeah, yeah, yeah. I gotta go."

And this is what he later told me . . .

He went early on a Sunday morning, and the address seemed to be down this isolated dirt road. He passed by a little shack with a big eighteen-wheeler parked on the side, parked in the muddy driveway, and walked up to the front door. Instead of address numbers next to the door, there was a picture of a spotted owl in a red circle with a red slash across the owl.

Bark knocked on the screen door and a big Lab ran up and barked from the other side. A large man with a wild black beard and a gut walked out into the kitchen with a pair of old jeans on. And when he got to the door, Bark had to look way up because this was a big guy. A big hairy guy with hands like frying pans, thighs like ham hocks, arms like pythons.

Bark tried to gracefully look down and pass a glance over his pants, but the wrinkle didn't seem spectacular, so he figured on his penis being small like a regular white guy's.

The man scratched his underarm and yawned like a straight guy.

"Hi, I'm sort of lost," Bark told him, and told him who and what I was looking for.

The man said, oh yeah, there's a whole house of retired lesbians just down the road, over that big hill. About a mile away.

He asked Bark if he wanted a beer or some coffee, and Bark said yes
because he thought he might want to have sex. He hadn't had sex with
a stranger in over a week, and this could be like a really good gay
lumberjack kind of porn experience, and he'd be sure not to talk
about the plight of spotted owls.

Well, they didn't have sex. Just had some coffee and left in search of the *goddamned chocolate-eating alcoholic lesbians.* This is what Bark thought, and he said, "This is what is wrong with my life."

The turn into the driveway was only marked with an old silver mailbox facing the main dirt road. He drove up a long muddy way with occasional holes filled with gravel.

When he got up to the house, it was an old two-story peeling white house with a front porch. There was no screen door this time, so he just used the knocker.

Only wind chimes and spider plants answered him. No one came to the door even though there were a couple of late-model compact cars parked on what could pass for a lawn in front of the house.

He walked down the slope on the edge of the house and there were big

paint chips and empty liquor bottles strewn all the way down to a great big huge deck overlooking a small pond. But what amazed him was that there was a great big futon lying on the grass in front of the dying fire of a huge brick fire pit. There were three women passed out, maybe dead from lead poisoning.

No, he could see them breathing, and suddenly felt like an intruder. There were two women with large butts cuddled together. They had tits like two coke bags stapled to their chests. Bark held up one of the least-mutilated snapshots of Hooter I'd given him, and there, next to the cuddling women, passed out on her back was none other than Hooter *Mujer* clutching a large plastic bottle of water to her stomach because alcohol can suck your pussy dry.

It wasn't nearly so dramatic kidnapping Hooter *Mujer* the second time. Just with the dead weight she was so heavy. He considered putting her in the backseat, but it was only a tiny white two-door and she was six feet tall. He could barely fold her into the front seat.

It was an hour's drive back to the city and with all the liquor bottles strewn around the grounds of the house and the pharmaceutical smell of this woman, he didn't figure on her waking up the way she did while they were driving.

"Hey, what is this?" She groggily lifted her head and looked around. "Why the *fuck* can't people leave me where I am?" I didn't tell bark that Hooter had a pretty vulgar mouth when she drank. "*Fuck you!* [hic] *Fuck* you! Stop this motherfuckin' car!" She banged and slapped on the window.

"Hey, hey, this is a rental car, take it easy!" He tried to hold her wiry arms down and drive at the same time.

"Just let me the fuck out right here, damnit [hic], shit!"

"I can't, I can't. Look, what Tomato did was wrong, I'll grant you that, but for some goddamned lesbian reason, Tomato's in jail on suspicion of murdering you and we've got to help her, let 'em know you're really alive."

"That's what this is all about? Well, good, goddamn, motherfucker! Let her rot in there, goddamn it, motherfucker!"

"You mean, you knew she was in jail for murdering you?"

"Of course [hic], she doesn't know how *we* live."

"What? How *who* lives?"

"She's a goddamned straight girl, doesn't [hic] know how to hang with us lesbians."

"Look, I'm not entirely sure what went on between you two, and I don't really care about this lesbian hairball stuff anymore. I just want my car back, I want to go home and stop taking care of that horrid cat, that's all, and that's not gonna happen until they find you're alive."

"Yeah, look motherfucker, I'm alive. Now let me go, shit damn [hic] motherfucker."

Her head was lolling all over her neck and he wasn't sure whether she was getting ready to throw up or say something else meaningful.

"Look, if you're going to get sick, open the window. I can't stand the smell."

She indignantly raised her head up and said with a hiccup, "I don't [hic] vomit, mister. Hey, what's your fucking name, anyway, goddamned motherfucker?"

"Bark."

"Well [hic] Bark, it's best for you to stay out of the lesbian world. You don't know what you're into."

"Look, don't patronize me. I know this goddamned lesbian stuff all too goddamned well. I used to have a sister who was a lesbian, and then she ran off to become a nun somewhere because that's what guilty Catholic lesbians do."

"Oh yeah? [hic] What's her name? I've probably fucked her. I've fucked just about every woman in San Francisco, if I may say so."

"As far as I know she was never in San Francisco, so I'm sure you never heard of her. Besides, I highly doubt you're her type."

"[hic] Oh, honey, I've fucked plenty of women who said I wasn't their type. Curious little girls with husbands named things like Brandon or Lester. See you don't know shit about lesbians."

"Well, I don't know where my sister ended up. Family trouble, I was sent off to Texas as a kid and she ran off to do nun service somewhere. Her name's May—and don't say 'may I blah blah blah.' We said it all the time when we were kids."

"Yeah, well, let me the goddamned [hic] fuck out of here—"

And then she projectile vomited and he tried to pull over, open her window or stop her, and just as they were barely out of the long, ragged driveway, they swerved into a tree, and that's all he remembers.

And she wasn't anywhere to be found when the ambulance found him.
He didn't even know how the ambulance knew to save him on such a
deserted road. One of the ambulance drivers said something about
getting a dispatch coming in from a CB radio like from a truck or
something.

They checked him for a concussion and he was fine.

He visited me to tell me all this.

"Well, didn't you go back to see if her friends at the house knew
where she was?" I asked him desperately.

"Yeah, yeah, I did. Even they don't know where she is."

"And you believe them?"

"Well, yeah."

"But wait, how could you have let her get away?"

"Look bitch, get off my back. As far as I can see there's been
nothing in it for me from day one. I'm stuck in a clan of the cave
bear house in San Francisco looking for a man with a big dick while
I'm trying to save your sorry ass. I could've died."

"You weren't even out of the driveway, yet. You didn't almost die.
Besides, you're looking pretty damn healthy these days."

0-0259-

"Yeah, well you weren't there. I saw a light. It was so peaceful and welcoming . . . so I started going toward the light. I heard a deep, booming voice and it said, 'Wait, son, you aren't done. You must fulfill purpose. Like write a book on 101 revenge techniques.' And then somehow I was yanked by my golden life thread back into my body."

Tomato covered her face with both hands and shook her head.

"Look," Bark continued, "I don't care how I die next time—"

"Next time?"

"Yeah, I don't care how I die next time, I just don't want to choke on a ham sandwich. And don't let me be buried in a piano. Enormous is having to get a cherry picker crane to lift you off your third-story perch. Don't talk to me about fat. I'm the one with three different kinds of meat carcass in your refrigerator. Remember, if God didn't want us to eat animals he wouldn't have made them out of meat.

"I've got the answer to my fat. I'm going to eat my way out. That's right, eatin' got me into it and eatin's gonna get me out. I've got tapes that explain to me about the metabolism rate. The key is insulin and glucagon. One is a sugar transfer from blood into the cell and tells fat to store, and the other shuts off the insulin receptors and encourages fat metabolism. Carbos flood the system with insulin thus, sugar transfer and fat storage. You should eat

60g of protein, 20g fat, 10g carbs. MEAT baby! YOU are a carnivore—get into it! Gatherers are meek and fat, while hunters are, well, aggressive and fat. Who cares, it's kill or be killed. Let the meek inherit the earth after we get done using it. There is still room in this diet for fake ice cream. It's your choice, but if you choose wrong don't bother crossing the Donner pass with me.

"Hey, why're you looking like that over there on your side of the glass, huh? You kinda remind me of Karen Black in that gremlin movie. You know, where she's blurry eyed, sitting on the kitchen floor stabbing a knife into the floor between her legs.

"Well, that cross-eyed Karen Black look is a good look to have for fighting fat. Fighting fat is war, and war is hell. Just don't go into battle all happy like the Pillsbury Dough Boy . . .

"Yeah, don't let me be buried in a piano. I'm going to fill the house with clocks to remind me that time is slipping away and I want the clocks to stop when I die, and then I want my dog to howl next to my gravestone until *he* dies."

I'd been meditating on a brand new scratch on the Plexiglas partition and snapped out of my boiling savage daze when he stopped. "Yeah, yeah, whatever. Listen," and I asked him what are we gonna do next and he said nothing. He actually said "nothing," he didn't just sit there.

"Look, I go to trial in less than a month. Isn't there something we can do to prove she's alive? Can't we get her prints from the car or have the vomit analyzed to prove it's hers?"

"Uh, I don't even know if you can do that . . ." Bark looked down, with an uncharacteristic kind of shame. He started to tremble just a little bit. And when he looked up he was looking right through me, through the wall behind me. It was vaguely familiar. "Plus, I have such a problem, I mean like a *serious* problem with vomit. It was a red-wine vomit. Kind of reminded me of something scary I vaguely remember from when I was a kid . . . Something . . . But I had to, I just had to, you know, clean it all out. *Immediately.*"

I felt my life force try to leave my body and go elsewhere more promising, because it's all about location, location, location. I threw my head down and started banging it on the table. "I'm doomed. I'm soooo doomed."

Bark was still staring catatonically past me, so I just waved good-bye. "Yeah, well Flam, never mind anymore. You might as well keep the apartment. You can sell the bike. Pink slip's under the bed. See ya, sunshine."

He couldn't even say good-bye. I don't know how long he sat there after I was gone, but I didn't hear anything, nothing, nada, from the outside for the next two months.

Eight months. I'd been a Zucchini Girl in Zucchini Cave for eight months.

I didn't care about anything anymore. Speaking to Veronica on the phone once a week was my one highlight, the only thing I had to live for. Since I didn't care about myself anymore, I finally relented, let Veronica call me Betty, and even let Big Bob Zadora call me whatever she wanted. Hell, who cares. I'd play telephone horsie with a cartoon Veronica if it helped to pass the time. Acting and feeling like an ennui-filled New Yorker had serious disadvantages. I couldn't even enjoy *Mary Poppins* the other night when it was on TV.

Was there absolutely nothing left to believe in?

No. I would be the best damn Betty that telephone Veronica had ever seen. I told her so, too. I said, go ahead. Bring it on. As long as I don't drink too much, you won't be disappointed.

Veronica sent some hair bleach, but prisoners weren't allowed to have such things, lest we should realize how life sucked and gulp it all down in a dramatic flourish. So, one Saturday night Sister May bleached my hair for me.

I never told Veronica how, with the new dark circles forming under my eyes, it really made me look like an old and bitter Baby Jane, sending a letter to *da-dee.*

Oh, Big Bob made fun of me and my special little relationship with telephone-Veronica, but I didn't care. We all have our quirks. Our little baggage. Some drag it along in trash bags while others carry it in leather cases with brass buckles.

I was in my cell, lying on my bed frantically trying to smother myself with a pillow when Sister May came in and cheerfully said, "Tomato! You've finally got visitors! Come on!"

I hadn't had a visitor for over two months.

"Why don't you finally change out of that, that . . . Thing." She wrinkled her face. "Don't you have a dress or something a little more cheerful than that old examination gown?"

Two. I was wearing two examination gowns. One in front and one in back to cover my hind side. I didn't care about fashion anymore. I didn't care about hair care or personal hygiene.

And because of this, my cellmates made me put my mattress on the floor over in the corner.

"Come on, hurry. They're waiting."

And Sister May rifled through my drawer to find some overalls for me to put on. "Oh, and here's a nice, bright T-shirt."

I pushed my feet into my sneakers, and crushed down the backs of them like slippers. I shuffled behind Sister May and followed her down the halls, past the C-section, and through the woods to the visiting room.

Waiting for me on the other side of the Plexiglas were sitting my New York gallery lawyer who blew impersonal kisses, and hovering at his side was my nervous-looking car-crash fog. Tule.

SHE'S NOT a LESBIAN

SHE'S BRITISH.

"Hi, sweetheart! Couldn't find time to shave this morning, huh?" My cheerful lawyer waved as if from the pages of a moving magazine. I hadn't seen a good suit in such a long time, or even a man in a shirt without a faint sweat stain around the collar. The prison officials who occasionally visited didn't exactly feel like they had to dress in their Sunday's finest to visit us girls.

I pulled back the chair, smoothed down the rear of my examination gown, and sat down. "Look, Mr. Boy, don't," I sluggishly pointed to him and tried to dramatically wipe my nose with the back of my hand. "Don't call me, uh. . . What did you just call me?"

He cheerfully raised his eyebrows and looked around for the answer. "Oh, I don't know, sweetheart?"

"Yeah, yeah. That's it. Don't call me sweetheart, princess, Betty, sweet pea, little girl, none of it. Just call me what I tell you to, okay? Okay?" I tossed a thick dreadlock of matted hair over my shoulder. It went thud. "Call me, uh, call me Mad Dog," I said. "Or big girl."

"Okay, big girl—"

"—wait, never mind. Big girl doesn't sound as good as I thought. Call me medium girl. Yeah, call me medium girl or call me Mad Dog."

He held up his hands. "Whoa, sorry!" And chuckled. His teeth were too white to be in my life right now and I squinted.

"You know." I dully poked at the Plexiglas. "You could've learned a lot by watching just a *Matlock* episode or two. You left me in here to rot in this shit hole."

"Oh, this place isn't bad at all. Brand new, in fact, and we had to pull quite a few strings to get you in here—"

"An experimental halfway-house prison for months of lame psychological observation? I'm worse now than when I got here."

"Well, it's better than being stuck in a *state* prison because you couldn't make bail."

"You didn't even give me a chance at bail."

"Due to the nature of the crime, you wouldn't have been able to afford my fee as well as your bail."

I snorted because I was disgusted but helpless and gross in a phlegmy, "love me anyway" kind of thing. I turned to Tule. "—And what's *she* doing here?" Tule didn't have good taste or anything, in fact she was a living, breathing, walking *Glamour* "Don't," but she still looked surreal sitting on the other side of me, enveloped in her own personal mist. Although it was covered with little white pills and the arms were a bit short, her colorless blazer wasn't wrinkled or stained, which seemed a miracle to me. If fluorescent lights can make even a small child look haggard while trying on a little skirted swimsuit, you can imagine how it shows every laundry mistake ever made, especially in the unforgiving atmosphere of civilized retribution. But what I envied most about Tule wasn't her freedom. No. It was how her hair had a bit of that frizziness of being freshly washed that same morning.

From my side of the Plexiglas, I couldn't smell anything with my own heavy clan-of-the-cave-bear musk going on, but I wanted to imagine that she smelled like perfume, a special soap from any drugstore, or even deodorant, as her face was a little shiny with perspiration. I would've been glad to smell anything that wasn't prison-issue deodorant soap or the industrial antiseptic cleaner we mopped the prison down with.

My lawyer clasped his hands together and leaned forward with an even bigger smile and I flinched because I couldn't even remember the last time I gave a damn about flossing. Flossing was from another era altogether and I suddenly understood why old people sometimes don't even give a damn about remembering their kids' names. He said, "Well, that's why we're here! What I'm trying to tell you, is—"

But I couldn't let him finish because I couldn't get past his teeth, his happy private-shower life, or his forgetfulness. "—hey, how can you make it in New York being so goddamn perky? It's not right. You're supposed to talk in a quick, coffee-nervous way like you're about to hang up to take another call, complain about New York, talk about how the weather sucks, how busy you are . . . not blow kisses. It's just not . . . What's that word?"

"What word?"

"Oh, natural. It's not natural, I tell ya."

"What's not natural, uh, Miss Mad Dog."

" 'Mizzz,' " I sluggishly corrected. "Call me 'Mizzz.' "

"Well, what's not natural?"

"Acting like that and being from New York," and I leaned forward and opened my eyes until they almost popped out and fell on the table. "Look at me. This," and I pounded on my chest with my hands and rubbed my hands over my matted hair, "this is what ennui looks like when you turn the light on too fast."

He wagged his little lawyer finger at me and snorted a chuckle. "Oh, you are a funny one, aren't you?" He put his palms on the table and opened his eyes wide like a surprised cartoon and enunciated every word, "—so, listen, Miss Chitlin here—"

"—Wait." I looked at Tule. "Your name's 'Chitlin'? Tule Chitlin?" She ignored me and nervously glanced at my lawyer. I repeated her

0-0271-

name over and over and started laughing. Even the guard had a smile on his face.

But the humor in her name was like pearls on a pig and my perky New York lawyer didn't get it. "Come, come, now listen: I have very, very good news for you."

I sat up when I saw actual New York irritation flash across his face and he continued, "Tule here was the main witness against you."

"What!" I jumped up so fast the chair fell backwards.

"Yes, now calm down, calm down," he talked slowly as if I were retarded and used his hands to show what calm down looked like. "There, there. Now, Miss Chitlin here has recanted her testimony against you and therefore you'll be free to go as soon as we file the paperwork."

I stood there, leaning against the Plexiglas, just quietly looking at her. As the fluorescent lights burned the fog away, suddenly I was no longer blindfolded and helpless in the haunted house. I saw the pullies making the doors slam shut, saw the strings shaking the chandeliers, and watered down catsup pouring forth from the faucets.

"But why?" I begged her. "Why? Would you do such a thing?"

And of course I knew why. It was stupid of me to ask, but I'm always asking the colors of the garage doors in stories, so I wanted to know everything.

"Well," and it was the first time I ever heard her speak, "I just want to say I'm really sorry. . ." She looked at my lawyer and he nodded for her to continue. She looked down at her lap as if she couldn't even see that far, and told me the whole story. "We just wanted to teach you a lesson," and Tule Chitlin burst into minute water droplets of tears and reached in her purse for a tissue and a tube of lipstick.

"We?" I asked, and I looked at my lawyer, "don't tell me you have something to do with this?"

"No, no, no," she waved her hand, blew her nose and said, "Hodie and I. Well, it was only supposed to be a little joke. Just to get you a little harassed by a visit from the police, maybe get a little ink on your fingertips . . . But I had no idea how big everything would get. It just got away from us . . ." She uncapped the lipstick, twisted it up, stretched her lips under her teeth and passed a little shaky orangey pink color over them, put the cap back on, jammed it back in her purse, cleared her throat and continued . . .

"It was her idea after you left her by the side of Route 1. When she got a ride from the side of the road to her friends' house, nearby, she wanted to learn you a lesson. So she called me from their place and had a little plan.

Ʊ-0273-0

"She said to call the police when you got back in town and I could drive by and take down your tag number . . . Say I'd been walking along the beach and witnessed someone throwing a body over the cliff and that when I climbed up to get closer, I saw a funny-colored Lexus 4x4 driving away—"

"—champagne," I corrected her.

"Huh?"

"It's not 'funny-colored,' it's champagne-colored."

"Okay, I was to say that I saw a champagne-colored Lexus 4x4 driving away, and that I just happened to get the tag number.

"I said it wouldn't work, but when I saw you at the Mild Side West later that afternoon, I called the cops from there with your tag number."

My perky New York lawyer filled in the gaps:

And from there, the cops traced the car to Bark Flammers, a longtime suspected hit man. And since Bark had thought I was trying to frame him for a sloppy murder to avoid paying him to do the job, he'd told them all my revenge plans and techniques.

Even though Bark didn't have a good alibi that morning, there was a record of a highway patrolman stopping to check on the Lexus by the side of the road. In his log, he'd recorded the tag along with the driver's license name and number.

So although that firmly left Bark in the clear, they didn't tell him this, and leaned heavily on him to cough me up like a hairball.

Bark had even given over the note about my borrowing the car, which was written on the back of Hooter's restraining order against me. And between his story of my hiring him to murder Hooter, the traces of blood from her nose in the car, and the testimony of all the people in the neighborhood who'd witnessed all my flamboyant acts of revenge against her, including the damning eyewitness account of my kidnapping Hooter in front of the Chihuahua man . . . It was a scary avalanche. Surprising I wasn't still stuck in my own little air pocket, smoking Lucky Strikes, and disinfecting my wounds with my own urine, some dog spit, or the squishy broken hearts that lined the ghetto streets of San Francisco.

Amazing I wouldn't be crossing my hairy legs in the electric chair.

And when my perky lawyer was through, he sat back and patted his stomach and smiled like he'd just eaten my last meal. "I've filed the papers for your release and you should be out in no time at all. So there. All's well that ends well!"

I was stunned. I had no idea how thick and rich and chocolatey the case had been against me. No fucking idea. I looked over to Tule and started slowly, "But why. . . If it was all getting out of hand, why didn't you both come forward and say I never killed Hooter? That she was alive?"

"Because once the police told us you'd hired a hit man, Hodie wasn't going to come out of the countryside until you were safely convicted, so we figured it was supposed to be this way and just went with it." Such an utterly Californian approach to framing people.

"And you would've gotten away with it too, if it weren't for us pesty kids, huh?"

"What?"

"Nothing. But I only hired Bark to help me come up with better ways of getting her back for breaking my squishy little bitter heart."

"Well, yeah, I know that now, Bark went to your lawyer to help you out. And your lawyer told me that Bark said it was all just a little misunderstanding between you two."

"Yeah . . ." I shook my head and looked at the table. "One hell of a little misunderstanding." I picked my chair up off of the floor and sat back down. I breathed in and I could feel the circles under my eyes returning to their smooth natural cardboard color, and I smiled to myself. I looked back at her because there was one more thing I didn't understand about the color of the garage door or her orangey pink lipstick . . . "So, who sent the postcard?"

"You mean the one that said Tomato was here?"

"Yeah. Who sent it?"

Tule looked away from me again. "Well, one night I was out there in the country with them and we all got really shit-faced, and one of Hodie's friends there thought it would be a real gas to send it to you."

"Real gas? Is that a special way you all talk together?"

"Excuse me?"

"Never mind."

"Oh—I get it. Yes, well, we were so drunk, it seemed like a good idea at the time. To tease you a little bit."

"Yeah, well this is all a great big touché." And I stopped short of telling her to go fuck herself and the horse she rode in on.

My lawyer leaned forward earnestly, like he wanted to point out what we'd learned. "Good. It's very good that you're not bitter. It's better to get a fresh yogurt out of the fridge and start over."

Yogurt? I looked at him, about to ask him what the fuck was he talking about and then I thought the better of that, too, because my own metaphors didn't run much faster than his. In fact, they were *behind* his yogurt, getting slippery and rotting, and I turned back to Tule. "But why uh . . . Why did you finally come forward? What inspired this . . . Almost spiritual uh . . . Merciful gesture of forgiveness?"

And with that familiar look I'd once seen in my own eyes, Tule clenched her fists in her lap and said through her teeth, which now had traces of orangey pink lipstick on them, "Because when Hodie stayed down in the country, she called me every day. Every day she told me she loved me, and me only. *'Baby one'* she even called me . . ." Tule's jaw was trembling and it made her voice shake. "And out of the blue, she just stops calling me . . . I haven't heard from her for over two months, *not one single thing.* She must think she can just drop me for another woman like that [snapped her fingers], so fuck her and her little plans, too."

Before I could suggest she sit, look out the window at some pretty green trees, and feel her angry feelings in a safe place, Tule got up in a huff and stomped out of the room to blow somebody else's house down.

Yeah, the postman rings twice, but not necessarily at the same house anymore.

My lawyer got up and blew me a kiss. "I'll be in touch!" And then he was gone in a rush of scary ending music that finally explained to me that the orangey pink lipstick was to keep sailors from crashing to their deaths.

E "COME-EAT-ME" CHAIR ALONG WITH THE "COME-FUCK-ME" PUMPS.

                              really
I really hate good-byes, so I won't go over them again here about
leaving the prison and saying bye Big Bob, Sister May, and the
Baby Chick and Snake girls in my cell. Suffice it to say, I packed
my stuff, reluctantly said good-bye to my fun house friend, which
went a little something like this:

Big Daddy Bob: "See you around, Snatch."

Me: "You've been swell, Big Daddy Butt. Hey, what's your real
name, anyway?"

Big Daddy Bob: "You keep your nicknames to yourself and I'll
keep my business to myself. Here, give me a hug."

Me: "Whoa—no dice. Don't touch the merchandise."

Big Daddy Bob: "Merchandise? Looks more like trash day."

And I went on to try and market my life like Garth Brooks and
get the most I could get. Which wouldn't send your kids to a
community college for a semester.

Encouraged by my short New York gallery dealers, my perky
New York lawyer set up a little press conference and he was
concerned that my roots were growing in. I said, don't worry, it
adds a touch of cheap, hard-core prison reality.

When you're in jail, you can't keep up with stuff like hair dye touch-ups, tweezing your eyebrows, or shaving your legs. I hadn't shaved in such a long time, and Big Bob said that all I had to do was iron a pleat down the middle and they'd look like slacks.

Anyway, remember when Oprah lost about sixty pounds and pulled a little red wagon overflowing of beef fat to show what sixty pounds of fat looks like? I wanted to be an inspiration and wheel out my own little red wagon and show how much weight I'd lost in jail. But since I'd only lost ten pounds, before the press conference I put five guinea pigs in the wagon and wheeled it out before I answered any questions, but its significance was **lost because the** guinea pigs were so short you couldn't even see them over the edge of the wagon.

So off I went to be the Betty to my telephone-Veronica.

She opened the door with a shiny black helmet of heavily gelled Veronica hair and I felt fear. Fear like there's a spittin'-mean raccoon going through the trash outside your tent, but now ... Now you can hear it fumbling with your tent zipper and you're naked and you think, hope, (—*wait*—) that it's gonna rape you, 'cause boy, you sure got a perty mouth.

Oh, it's not that telephone-Veronica was ugly, she was just covered with pancake makeup and eyeliner and stood before me and I tried to photograph pieces of her with my mind so I could look at them later without staring, unlike men. I was determined to give this piece a chance. I was trying to wait and see if things would click the way they did when we used to talk on the phone during my prison days when I had only a spider and my talking image in a fun house mirror to get me through.

After she kissed me hello on the cheek, told me to sit down, put a vodka martini in my hand, and plopped herself on my lap, she talked about all the problems of her old lovers, cried on my shoulder that she just wanted to be taken care of. I asked for a couple more martinis.

She was giving me the creeps now that she was real flesh and blood, I didn't feel like giving in but I did.

She wanted to go out for a light supper, so we went down the street to a place filled with people in their early twenties who wore Jimmy Hoffa platform shoes, drank martinis, and were never quite sure of the difference between Audrey and Katharine Hepburn. Now that I was almost thirty, I felt superior because at least I was alive when Audrey died.

I had lightly sauteed spinach greens with walnuts, and don't remember what she had, even though she kept trying to feed me with her goddamned pitchfork. I kept saying no thank you, and when we were done, she sat right next to me and put her head on my shoulder. I drank my entire glass of water. Slowly.

"You don't like PDAs, do you?" Veronica asked.

I tried to look down at her but it was difficult because she was right under my chin. "Excuse me?" I asked.

"You know, 'public displays of affection.' "

"Uh, no, I'm not much for that kind of thing because I can't focus on your eyes. For instance, I'm looking at the waiter right now." And this was true, because the waiter came right over and asked if we needed anything. "The check will be fine," I said, and he turned around to tally it up.

Veronica got up and sat back across from me and winked. When the waiter turned around, he dropped the leatherette check-thing halfway between her and me. Veronica pushed it toward me, pursed her lips, and said, "You don't mind, do you?"

I said no even as I was beginning to hate her.

Even though my breasts are big enough to unfurl over any decent balcony, I found her tits big, intimidating, and uncontrollable with the consistency of water. They flowed over my hands like fountains and I didn't know whether to pick them back up or use a paper towel. They weren't like Hooter's unassuming little ones. Big tits demand a whole lot of attention, and can give anyone performance anxiety, because no matter how masterfully you caress big tits, you always look cheap and vulgar, like the person with the tits is just waiting for you to move on to the next thing/because that's how I've felt so many times.

All my first-time sex with someone new sucks, sucks bad, and this was even worse. At a crucial moment after lots of kissing and poking, there was a very long, awkward pause when we were both on our backs staring at the ceiling, waiting to see who was going to get on top of who first and do all the work. After ten or fifteen minutes with neither one of us moving or looking away from the ceiling, I gave in because it was obvious I was going to have to get on top to get this over with. Besides when I thought about it, I didn't really want to give in to her anyway, and so feeling like something between a pillow queen and a stone butch, I sighed, rolled over on top of her, and tried to get a good rhythm and blues thing going.

After about ten seconds, I realized that being a top was just too much fucking work. As soon as she made some happy gurgling sounds, I dropped on top of her. "My arms hurt," I complained and rolled back over onto my own back where the room started to spin.

"Oh, that's okay," she answered back in that overly understanding, singsong tone of voice I myself had used so, so many times before. And just like you're supposed to do, she then affectionately pulled a curl from my forehead and let it spring back.

It made me shudder now to hear one of the oldest lines for men used on *me*, and I found myself frantically explaining, "Well, wait. This doesn't usually happen. Must've been the alcohol. Really." I'd also heard this *so, so* many times before.

She just nodded and stroked my hair in that Professionally Understanding Way. Apologizing all the way, I hoisted myself up, picked through all of our clothing on the floor, and started to put my pants on. That's when she sat up halfway, put her hands on her hips, and insisted that I go down on her. I cringed, but I figured I'd be better off than if I said no, so with one pant leg on, I went ahead so I could leave, but I couldn't even find her clitoris. I hated that. No Mexican hat to dance around and I hated feeling like I was floating in the endless space of her anonymous pussy.

It was so much work snarfin' around for truffles that just weren't there, and I just wanted to wipe my mouth and go home. And she wanted me to stay the night. I wanted to sleep in my own bed. She pouted, squirmed, and writhed in the sheets, and whined that she wanted more from our relationship.

I looked at her and clapped my hands together. "I'm sorry, I've really *got* to go now. So, *sooo* many things to do, you know, coming back from prison and all," and I skipped out of her bedroom.

As I reached out for the front door she yelled, "Hey, where did you learn how to have a relationship, anyway?"

I poked my head back through her bedroom door. "Excuse me?"

She dramatically turned toward me in the bed. "I said, where did you learn to have a relationship *anyway?*"

"Oh." I tapped my teeth with my fingers. "Relationship?" Shaking my head and leaning against the doorway I cheerfully answered, "I didn't want any relationship."

"Then what did you think *this* was?" And she ripped the sheets off her body and narrowed her eyes at me.

"Oh, I don't know." I drew circles with the toe of my boot and exhaled, "Veronica, I just wanted to have fun. You know. . . sit back, stroke my comb-over, light up a clove and have you lift up your shirt for me and dance like a Vegas showgirl. Is that too much to ask?"

And apparently she didn't appreciate my cracker-dry sense of humor about all of this hideous role playing, because Veronica screamed "pig" and threw a very heavy shoe at me.

"Okay, okay." I waved good-bye. "Why don't we just take some time to think about everything. It's all moving sooo quickly." And in seconds I had my hand on the front door and was gone. Gone and cold-sober as soon as I hit the night air.

I would've felt terrible, but I was free, white, and twenty-one.

I went home and waited until she was at work the next day so I could break up with her on her answering machine.

I had no idea how cleansing it could be to break up with someone. To be the one who's dying to say just shut up already.

And when she tried to call me a couple of times in the middle of the night, very gently I reminded her what I'd gone to jail for.

I never heard from her again.

And I went back home to my porn-movie life with Bark. He was sticking around because Kris and Bootsy didn't really want him back in Texas since they needed his room. Bootsy had finally gotten pregnant, and was due in the not too distant future.

When I told him about my evening, he said that since I'd been in jail and rode a motorcycle, it'd be generally expected that I be butch now. Pay for coffee. Open doors. Take charge. Make decisions. Change tires. Back down in arguments. But where, I asked Bark, where was the upside for me?

"You sound like those men in the seventies who hated feminism," Bark said. And then he explained that bedding women is a lot of work because you have to get the right color roses, set the table, fold napkins into swans, light candles, pop open a good cabernet. He said it can be worth it if you really want someone to talk to afterwards.

"But men are different," he told me. "Having sex with other men is like eating over the kitchen sink."

"Are you ever going to go back to women? You know, get married?" I asked him.

And he said, "Why the hell would I want to get married? I'm shallow enough as it is."

He was so happy to have his champagne-colored Lexus back, we spent many evenings cruising up and down Union Street, San Francisco's heterosexual mecca, pointing and laughing at all the straight people. We also tried to talk about life so we both wouldn't feel so vapid.

"You know," he said one night as we were driving around. "That's the sad, horrible truth. That we are what we look like and what we smell like. And when we go up to heaven, there'll be God, sitting there and smoking cigarettes because He can, and He'll tell us to come into The Phlegm, instead of The Light."

"The Phlegm?"

"Yes. You'll understand when you're older."

Q-Q288-A

"But I thought that when you died before, you heard something about The Light?"

"I've made a mistake. It was The Phlegm."

A few local papers picked up the story of my case, and a big New York publisher even approached me to write a book about my experience, but I refused to sell out. No way José, not the life for me, because after the glitter fades I'd have nowhere left to go but the Hollywood Squares. I'm an artist, I told them, and had many more fake penises to make. Go talk to Bark, I said. He has a book of 101 revenge ideas, and so they did.

Things soon quieted down. And without a *cheat and die* cause, all my admirers went back to saving Mumia Abu Jamal.

And being self-righteous soon made me run out of money, so I eventually contacted Purse Book Publishing about putting my prison diet on every checkout counter in America.

They gave me a hundred-dollar advance and put the picture of me with the guinea pigs on the cover of my *Mad Dog's Ten-Pound Prison Diet!* It was displayed with all the calorie counters at grocery store registers. So I did readings at checkout lines, sometimes spontaneously when I was buying milk or cat litter, to promote my book with the belief that people will pick up anything but bad poetry. They'll read candy wrappers before they read bad poetry.

Bark did well, and eventually moved to New York. When I "accidentally" saw him on one of the twelve talk shows I watch each day, promoting his book, which is called *Eat Me*, I got so depressed about not only ruining Hooter's life, but my own.

I wasn't exactly skipping across the streets with enthusiasm. I wanted to run away in slow motion to a land where flowers grew like ghetto trash, a place where persuasive long-distance phone companies couldn't find me and change my mind, a place where I'd never have to reach my potential. A place where I'd get the feeling I still had at least one foot on the ground, was still listed in the phone book, and paying taxes. Instead, I was leading the kind of ghetto life with skittish, sweaty people backing into each other without saying excuse me, and I could be found facedown at my desk with a Bic pen sticking out of my spinal cord, five bucks missing from my pocket.

For the first time in my life, I was inspired to call the psychic hotline.

When I got her on the line, I asked the psychic if I had a future.

What did she see? I asked while she leafed the fortune-telling files of her mind . . . And after many false starts like a car on a frozen morning, she finally cleared her throat and said, "Chairs."

"Chairs?" I coughed, my voice fighting past my sinking heart.

"Why, yes. Chairs."

I didn't say any more, because I figured she was for real and knew I'd given her someone else's credit-card number and was batting around my hopes for the future like they were half-dead mice.

I found the credit card on the ground at the gas station when I stopped to fill my bike with a few bucks in gas. The credit card didn't look run over, faded or old like Cher, so I figured someone had just dropped it. With one last dose of my coagulated adrenaline slogging its way through my veins, I stormed inside to the counter to go a little crazy and buy lots of things because I wasn't too worried about the recidivism rate. Bad things like Canadian cigarettes, maybe even a lighter in the shape of a cowboy boot.

I asked the aging Chinese cashier for these things. Canadian smokes, novelty lighters. But he didn't understand a word I said. He just shrugged and pointed out at my bike and held up three fingers.

I looked down at the scuffed white Formica counter and all the shiny, sticky streaks from sliding things and money back and forth like textbook examples of capitalism. He slid my newfound credit card over a coffee ring and that's when I figured he knew everything. He was only pretending to not speak English so he could stall for time to call the cops . . .

And just as I was turning to make a skipping getaway to my bike, he flipped the credit card in his hand and swiped it through the little credit-card machine and started punching in numbers.

"Wait!" I shouted, "I, uh, have to get a few more things." And grabbing my chance at something more than a few dollars in gas for nothing, I quickly leafed through a stack of shrink-wrapped tapes on the counter where promotional American cigarettes should've been coupled with free novelty lighters. "Add this to my total," and not being famous for thinking particularly fast in a crisis, I lay down three copies of Tiffany's greatest hits and he rang it all up and handed me back the credit card as if it were mine.

After this episode, I wasn't really going to use the credit card again, especially when given three wishes by a rotting magic fish, I end up panicking and reaching for Tiffany in a crunch. You really can't trust people like me as part of any kind of social revolution or to even think clearly in the event of an accident. We're only good at holding the doors open and taking notes. And that's why I'd like to be hidden away in my own shack somewhere up in Montana with a whole arsenal and a compound named after myself; because no one can tell me Tiffany's a stupid move. I already know that.

Just chairs? She just had to know this was a bad credit card, or **maybe** they're like this with all their despondent callers.

Then I asked her whatever happened to a woman named Hooter, Hooter *Mujer?*

She was silent for a few seconds and finally she said Hooter had been in some kind of little accident months and months ago . . . perhaps an auto accident with a strange, grouchy man . . . And they'd been rescued by a passing neighbor . . . A lumberjack who hated spotted owls and now drove a huge truck . . . A big guy. *A big hairy guy with hands like frying pans, thighs like ham hocks, arms like pythons . . . A guy who was secretly in love with her . . . But during the accident, she'd hit her drunken head on the windshield and gotten short-term amnesia.* Not long term like in the soap operas.

Then the psychic said that he told Hooter that she was his wife and she said, "I *am?*" And he said, "Yeah." And he said, "Oh yeah, and you also like to wear my underwear," and she said, "I *do?*" And he said, "Yeah, and you like to give me blow jobs while I'm watching TV," and she said, "I *what?*"

And that most of their **conversations** were along those lines.

This psychic was good, so I asked her, "What about her friends who apparently live just down the road? Don't they ever see her and run up to her and tell her who she really is? That she's really a big, tall lesbian?"

And the psychic answered that yes, although Hooter sometimes sits out on the front porch drinking lemonade, her friends pass by in the car, too toasted to even notice her. And when they're driving that back road sober, it's usually in the dark.

"Oh my God! Will Hooter *ever* remember who she really is?" I asked in all-is-forgiven horror.

And again the psychic was silent a few seconds before coming up with, "Well, I see a pretty bright red box . . . Much like a cigar box . . . But there are no cigars. What's this? Chocolate? Bars and bars of chocolate. On each wrapper is printed, *'Devil Girl chocolate—eat it, it's bad for you.'* "

"*What?*" I asked, for I couldn't believe my ears.

"I'm sorry, but I see what I see. And I see this on a night table far into the future . . . Oh, dear . . . Your Hooter will be an old woman with a visitor . . . The visitor has brought her a box of Devil Girl chocolates and she suddenly realizes, or admits, who she is . . . and Hooter starts a laughing and a laughing because she's had a lot of fun in her amnesia. Pretty happy curling up on somebody else's lap for a change. "

So it looked like I should leave Hooter alone. If the road to hell is paved with good intentions, then the road to heaven is paved with bad ones. And if I'd just seen the clues before, I wouldn't have wasted my last precious psychic minutes on the phone putting it all together in my mind. See, as I now knew, it's a lot of trouble having to be in charge of everything. It's got to be awful tiring being a top, always yelling out directions like

"Lick my asshole!"

"Sit over there!"

Hooter opened doors, pulled out chairs, paid for drinks, lit cigarettes, offered her lap when all the barstools were gone, and did all the work in bed. She'd be whatever you needed without looking at you funny. Nothing shocked her, for she'd already been around the block and back for the next generation.

When s/m became all the rage, she accommodated the new girls who wanted to be treated like Victorian ladies in public and battered ten-cent Bangkok whores in bed. But Hooter once admitted that it got tiring hitting all of her girlfriends who dabbled in s/m. Remembering each woman's particular "safe" word and pain-level preference so they could play "scampering little rape victim" made her resentful for always having to play the Indian. One time she told me she was fisting this one girl, the girl's yelling "Harder! Harder! Harder!" and so Hooter pushes a little too hard and the girl screams in pain, jumps off the bed, cries, and says it's all over between them because she "hurt" her *too much*. I kid you not. And I even heard the story from the other side, too, and I had to change the subject.

0-0295

Why did she go along? Well, there's just something obliging about lesbian Texans, don't even waste your time trying to impose your fancy, big-city self-help books on them. They're doing just fine without our lonely-Saturday-night help. Besides, in San Francisco, saying you don't feel like going along with a little dirty talk or hot candle wax here and there is tantamount to having quiet, God-fearing sex with the lights out.

So a little amnesia and a big truck-driving alpha dog man for Hooter. She's the little cupcake for a man with hands like frying pans, thighs like ham hocks, and arms like pythons, a man who can hold up his end along with hers. It's not so bad to be the bottom. For her it's got to be quite relaxing for a change.

My friend Clarxn thinks amputation may be the next body-art rage, but I insist that the next big rage will be for straight white boys, and it won't be that drum-pounding, stick-passing, daddy-missing movement. No, it'll be when all these boys come home from work, slam brand-new, shrink-wrapped dildos on the kitchen tables and tell their girlfriends to strap up "because, Sweet Pea, things are gonna change around here."

Such a movement might prompt these receptive boys to have their own parade once a year. The girlfriends will have hands like frying pans, thighs like ham hocks, arms like pythons, and protectively march by their sides with bobbing plastic woodies so they don't get splashed by passing horses and buggies. The boys will

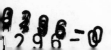

frantically wave at the audience. All will notice how the boys' hips move just a little freer than last year.

". . . Well, okay, your fifteen minutes are up . . . Perhaps you would like to pay for an additional ten?"

I didn't want to press my luck and go from the happy land of misdemeanor to the chilling land of felony. "Wait—just one more quick question, please."

"Hmmm . . . Okay, just this once."

"I know a girl named Big Bob. Big Bob Zadora. What's her real name?"

"Tiffany."

Tiffany? I'm telling you, the coincidences were just smothering me like a big pillow. "And is she really a spy for the prison company?"

But she didn't hear me . . . "Uh oh, wait, hold on now—the vision's coming back in—for you I still see . . . I still see a chair . . . A chair," and I could hear her pausing to move the phone a little and blow her nose. "Is it a chair? Hmm, no wait . . . I see a toilet seat, and it's up. Thank you for calling."

"A toilet seat and it's up?" My **voice cracked.**

"Yes, I'm sorry. We can only tell what little the spirits reveal to us ... And, my little friend, if they show us a toilet seat, who are we to question why?"

"But I'm not questioning why toilet seats are up as much as I'm questioning how you can see Hooter's whole, entire life, when I'm the one paying for this call and you're just leaving me here with toilet-seat visions—"

"—I'm sorry, dear, your fifteen minutes really are up."

And so was a toilet seat in my future.

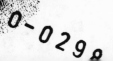

0-0298

Many things have changed since I became acquainted with lesbianism in the seventies at the age of eight. Like computers, it's a rapidly changing industry. Hairy chins and short fingernails are not enough anymore. Where only armpit hair and a little braless anger was once necessary to make a splash, now you have to grow stylish beards, and there are accessories like clitoral pumps to make clits as big as walnuts and Femme Conferences where femmes angrily discuss the rampant sexism between butches and femmes although the femmes still only—"uh oh"—have 75 cents for the pizza they ordered.

Now that the communists have folded and straight men are not only making even more money but winking at gay men in saunas, the new enemies are the poor, unsuspecting butches who didn't even see this coming because they were off at work trying to make enough money to cover the pizza. Uh oh, little butch girl, you'd better run and fast because not only does your femme have the whole world in her hand, she's got an Exacto blade.

I was hoping that making it this far would endow me with some kind of spiritual depth or something better than talking about a girl's tits with the expectation that I'll be willing and able to do something sexy with them once she pushes them into my face.

I'm whiny and tired of my own caustic voice and teen-age-boy approach to sexuality. Appropriate I guess that my future has a bitter, lonely toilet seat up in it. That's okay. I'm older now, and am used to the idea that most of the time you've just got to plow straight ahead. ⌇⌇⌇⌇Have faith you're in Vietnam for a reason.

Whether or not I'm a sarcastically optimistic thirty-year-old depends on the day of the week. But it's Friday and I know I'm at least a bit smarter. I'm working on it so that if I can avoid the minivans and make it to forty, I've earned The Right. The Right to the best parts of the chicken or The Right to one of those special seats in the front of the bus. And by then that may be all I need. Good thing, because Social Security will probably just be penny-candy money by then.

Until now, I hadn't changed much since the third grade when I lost the spelling bee because, for the life of me, I couldn't remember that "maybe" had a "y." I spelled it like "mabe." Mostly, I hated the word and stuck to a sharp and decisive "yes" or "no" that has often run my life into black or white gutters, totally unable to enjoy life in the gray area . . . the frumpy but ever faithful *perineum*.

The whole thing was somehow supposed to be ironic. I was supposed to wear huge sunglasses and it was all supposed to be okay in a funny-ha-ha kind of way that you cavalierly toss over your shoulder.

Like Isadora Duncan.

We must remember. Remember her by waving Bic lighters in the air and singing Lilith Fair dirges. We must remember how she died and never ever let it happen again./We must clap our hands to our mouths and remember that *there but for the grace of God go we.* Hey, haven't we been tossing our own fashionable scarves over our shoulders and just barely getting the ends caught in the turning wheels of the sports cars of our lives?

Because even when you've got the sunglasses and just the appropriate amount of ennui-fringed social conscience, and even with occasional glamorous flashes of clarity (that get more and more rare as you *finally* exit puberty at say, thirty), you're still bumping into the world. You have to be a person, you can't be a role. You have to be some*body* instead of some*thing.* Besides, that's *sooo* Andy Warhol. So L.A. So *Dance Fever.*

Even with all of our 7 Habits/Ten Commandments/12 Steps/and 39 Steps, most of the time you've just got to be a shivering naked little person. You can't pass Andy Warhol's corpse around so people will come to your party. No. From the football field, we all look alike in the stands. But of course we're not. We're like all those once-frolicking plastic-wrapped chickens under the buzzing lights in the grocery store. Vulnerable. Real. Individual. And subject to all sorts of infections.

Now that I'm thirty, and entering the gray area of my life, I finally believe that smoking can kill even me.

302-0

0-0302-0   0-0302-0
0-030

I once asked Bark how he could rim some guy without gagging and he said, "I don't know. Like dogs, men just seem to want to lick what they're about to fuck. You have to do it when you're so excited you can't think straight because something like rimming involves a *lot* of denial."

I get the lick-what-you-want-to-fuck thing, but I take it a little too far and want to fuck what I want to *become.*

The toilet seat's up.

And I want to be straight again for a little while. Bark Flammers once called me a lesbian who likes to suck dick and he's right. He says I'm like one of those vegetarians that craves steak once in a while. Again, he's right and I won't even bother pillaging and raping it for irony because I've got to move on and I'll be a totally different kind of straight girl.

But who in the hell wouldn't want to suck dick? And I feel the same way about shuckin' oysters, too. It was just time for a little mystery. A little stretchy-testicle mystery. I wanted to know a man well enough to hold a blow dryer or a cup of ice to his testicles and this time really pay attention to what happens.

A little mystery.

0-0303-

100% pure beef lesbians try and pretend they're grossed out by the whole "leaky penis" thing, and yet they keep getting big, leaky boy dogs who leave little yellow stains all over their hand-me-down lesbian furniture, and then they just love it when they figure out how to do that female ejaculation thing.

There was this hideous g-spot ejaculating movie where all these women are diddling themselves in a garishly lit living room, moaning and proudly squirting all over the place. I'm telling you, I was scared./ Very, very scared. Too scared to ever say a word.

★ Until now. I'm finally breaking the silence. ★

One skinny, creepy girl talked about **spooging** all over her wall by her bed at home and leaving it there to dry because she was so damn proud.

Too much. Too much information, I tell you. You're probably saying the same thing right now. But I want to share my terrifying fears like something gross I saw on the way to the forum. But sharing hideous visions never takes them away. It really just makes them live on like a bad infection.

That whole g-spot squirty-thing is just kind of ironic, isn't it? And kind of sad when you turn the volume way down and it all comes down to an old penis envy theory singing just a little off-key.

SO MANY COMPLICATED EMOTIONS in REGARD TO SQUIRTED wetness...

→ But that's kind of the best part, wouldn't you say? Kind of lets you instantly know you were doing something right, and you don't even have to be a rocket scientist. Perfect win-win situation.

Yeah, I'll be a totally different kind of straight girl.

Maybe I'll spend a couple of weeks and try to change a man, any man, obsess about my weight, and ask if my tube socks make me look fat, but I think I won't even wait around for the answer because I'll change my mind again and decide to become a straight white man instead. I'll want to smoke cigars with my big hair, play golf, buy property in San Francisco, and be a part of the decision-making process—say things like, "Hey, what's the bottom line?"

Wait'll they get a load of me at the Republican convention.

This marginalized stuff may look exotic across a crowded bar ten minutes before last call and it may gain you entry into a really cool, pissed-off group raising its fists, but it's still not enough. Not yet anyway, until sometime in 2000 when colored people outnumber white. But until that train comes 'round and we at least graduate high school knowing how to read, the NEA's not gonna pay any of us to cover ourselves in excremental chocolate because California already thinks thirty years of affirmative action was more than enough time to put our dresses on right and get in the goddamned car.

305-0

My toilet seat's up and it's time to fuck what I want to become and lick what I want to fuck. Time to live like an Elton John mondogreen song and live my life like a Ken doll in the wind. Say what you will but keep your judgment in your front pocket and tell someone else you're just glad to see them because even though I've only just begun, I've heard it all before.

With God as my witness, you won't catch me pissing on your leg and telling you it's raining. Why? Because it's high time to fall in love with a generic white boy who rides motorcycles, has underarms that smell like Old Spice, knows how to cry once in a while and when I mention therapy, in all sincerity he'll ask, "What's therapy?" And all I'll have to do to be considered good in bed is just say yes. Whenever I want, he'll finger-fuck me like a good little girl, and after, I'll happily slip on my special hairy knee pads and give him blow jobs. Maybe I'll actually look forward to swallowing again, as long as asparagus isn't involved. On Saturdays, maybe I'll strap one on and fuck him back, and he'll love me for it.

And on some Sunday night while we drink our dark beers, we'll talk about how fun it is going down on girls who know how to flail around and we'll rubberneck as all the pretty topless waitresses pass by.

If this were a novel, I'd end it with us curling up on the sofa during a *Matlock* Monday-night marathon. We'd quietly watch, smoke cigarettes, read piles of sexual advice columns, and eat ice cream all at the same time. And because we'll be buddies and buddies aren't paranoid, neither one of us will suddenly turn to other and ask . . .

What are you thinking?

And if this guy breaks my heart, it's back to the dogs for me. Where simple living is a salty hand, a good can opener, a nice cabernet, and thou.

Well, so there's my cautionary tale. Not real sure what the point was, so whatever you got out of it, you got out of it. It's the written equivalent of the Rorschach test. It is what it is. What you didn't get out of it wasn't there.

Live and be well.

0-0307

☆ LITTLE SHOP OF THINGS MONEY CAN'T BUY **BLOW OUT SALE**

THE EVIL JANITOR DOLL!!

He's finally here, your very own EVIL JANITOR Doll. The one you've been creaming about! Cute, cuddly and hours of fun! With all the quirky features of the real Evil Janitor.

ORDER NOW!

Educational and Fun!

Great for all ages!

only! $9⁹⁹

Call now for special bonus offer, a free pair of tin snips!! Wow!!

FAKE **GUN SOAP**

Clean your dirty little self with that pistol-whipped freshness.

MAKES A GREAT GIFT!

Don't Miss Out!!

Check it out!!

★ ★ ★ ★ ★

SPECIAL INTEREST

BUXOM LESBIAN in extremely bad mood, seeks anal-retentive little twirp to tie to basement piano, pump full of enemas and shout show tunes into ears. Serious inquiries only. Leave Message

GREASY, aging, balding, playboy with fancy car seeks young beautiful model type, to enjoy sinful nights painting the town and quiet days attending to sick wife. Must enjoy Bingo. Experience preferred.

Limited Time Only!! # HAIRY KNEE PADS *(for bisexuals)*

Sexy and soft, for hours of pleasure!

Welcome to the Wonderful World of Fellatio *and* Cunnilingus!

* Collect all 2 sets!!

Special! Oral sex tips hidden inside kneepad pockets —in case you forget!

*bi-coastal knee pads; with images of Golden Gate Bridge and Statue of Liberty

✂ -

☑ # YES! RUSH MY ORDER NOW!!!

NAME _____

STREET _____

CITY, STATE _____

ZIP, PHONE _____

Unfortunately we really can't send you this stuff. But it is fun to pretend, so fill out the card and wait by the mail box for the package you will never receive. Thank you for your support.

CHIHUAHUA IN A JAR!

NEW!

NO WALKING! NO FEEDING! NO ANNOYING BARKING!

Imagine having your very own *Chihuahua in a Jar!!* Sealed in formaldehyde so it's good as new, and better than living. A wonderful treat for the whole family! Don't miss out on this amazing offer. It won't last. *Call Now!*

And tomorrow's word is "Dacron."

Because until you can be completely, absolutely, unequivocally, and unflinchingly real, the only thing you can figure on doing is to take a Dacron approach to things and fake that your life is interesting because then maybe it will be. If you know what's good for you, you'll be demanding enough to not fake your orgasms, but you will fake how fascinating you are in a Dacron kind of way, especially if you're hanging out in the *perineum* of life and things haven't started to get interesting yet. It's a juggling act, like kids and family. Dog and girlfriend. Lesbianism and peace of mind.

Between "perineum" and "Dacron," you've got your work cut out for you.
My work here is done, I'm off to see the wizard . . .

They call him
John Jacob Jinkle Heimer Schmidt

His name is my name, too, because now that I'm thirty, you can call me whatever you want.

And don't you believe a word of what they say about me and those flying monkeys./I was simply looking for an old friend.
An Irish setter they call Billy.

MY GRATITUDE JOURNAL

God is Great, God is Good, and thanks for my friends/collaborators: Mark "Flammer Man" Lammers—special intellectual-property farm land that Kris Kovick and I routinely harvest. He gave and gave until he felt like gutting me with a plastic fork, but I know he cares/I also stole lines from "Cherry" Mary Starvus Stack, my stylish neighbor and friend, who loves me enough to stop vacuuming after 11 P.M. * When we ride on my motorcycle, she makes me laugh so hard, I have to pull over so we don't hit oncoming UPS trucks/Thanks to Sandra "Lady" May for a good time/and "Big Daddy" Bob Mecoy for letting me write it all down. He's the man with the plan, and a Southern accent in his hand. He IS Mistra' Know-it-all, and one of the only people I seem to cry like a baby in front of/Thanks to Paul "Meat Dog" Smith, my artistic collaborator who knows how to make Pagemaker howl like a middle-aged wolf on her wedding night/If life were a teen movie, Secret Agent Leigh Feldman would be the sexy guidance counselor with a heart of gold and a BMW roadster/"Swete" Pete Fornatale—you'd better start talkin' and fast, 'cause he just doesn't have that New York-kinda time/Ted Landry and the Pussycats: Maria Massey, Diane Tong, and Tia Maggini for hairspraying this frizzy mess/Robert Crumb for letting me use Devil Girl in the evil spirit for which it was intended/Dennis Caines for being a creative and sexy lawyer/Belinda Batcha (SignatureSoftware.com) for setting up my font/Ray Chipault at Underwood Photo Archives for saving my bacon/Emily Charles, Alex Hatch, Roseann Dial, Mark de la Viña, James Swanson for giving a Bette Davis-damn/Jean Sompayrac for kickstarting her bike and looking cool/Michael Dougan for inspiring me to remain a cartoonist/Janelle and Terri at Good Vibes for keeping this creepy celibate up to speed/A big, sloppy-dog thanks for my perpetually sunburned mom (Debby Reese) and my coffee-addicted sister (Elena Lopez), even though they pretend they're the "normal" ones/And thanks to all of you who wrote encouraging letters and helped me to make it past the Sophomore Jinx. I hope. OH!→ and A MAJOR thanks to MARTIN NOVELLi in N.J., who turned me onto Mysteries + RECEnt history in the FiRst place!